CPTW
11/11

D0284722

Outlaw

A NOVEL BY STEPHEN DAVIES

 CLARION BOOKS | HOUGHTON MIFFLIN HARCOURT | BOSTON   NEW YORK | 2011

CLARION BOOKS
215 Park Avenue South, New York, New York 10003

Copyright © 2011 by Stephen Davies
First American edition 2011
Originally published in the United Kingdom in 2011 by Andersen Press Ltd.

All rights reserved.

For information about permission to reproduce selections from this book,
write to Permissions, Houghton Mifflin Harcourt Publishing Company,
215 Park Avenue South, New York, New York 10003.

Clarion Books is an imprint of Houghton Mifflin Harcourt Publishing Company.

www.hmhbooks.com

The text was set in Fournier MT.
Book design by Sharismar Rodriguez

Library of Congress Cataloging-in-Publication Data
Davies, Stephen, 1976–
Outlaw / by Stephen Davies. —1st American ed.
p. cm.
Summary: The children of Britain's ambassador to Burkina Faso,
fifteen-year-old Jake, who loves technology and adventure, and thirteen-year-old Kas,
a budding social activist, are abducted and spend time in the Sahara desert with
Yakuuba Sor, who some call a terrorist but others consider a modern-day Robin Hood.
ISBN 978-0-547-39017-8
[1. Kidnapping—Fiction. 2. Survival—Fiction. 3. Brothers and sisters—Fiction. 4. Social
problems—Fiction. 5. Terrorism—Fiction. 6. Burkina Faso—Fiction. 7. Sahara—Fiction.]
I. Title.
PZ7.D2845Out 2011   [Fic]—dc22
2011009643

Manufactured in the United State of America
QFF 10 9 8 7 6 5 4 3
4500345699

This book is dedicated to Norbert Zongo (1949–1998),

who had the courage to take a stand against corruption

and paid for it with his life.

en.wikipedia.org/wiki/Norbert_Zongo

ACKNOWLEDGMENTS

Burkina Faso, West Africa, has been my home since 2001. Many thanks to my friends and neighbors there for sharing with me their lives, their proverbs, and their wonderful stories.

I am also grateful to my father-in-law, Neil Harrison, who introduced me to UCAVs (Unmanned Combat Air Vehicles), and to my lovely wife, Charlie, who introduced me to horses.

ᚩᚾᛖ

Jake Knight ran along the deserted towpath past Armley Mills and the industrial museum. It was two o'clock in the morning, and he was so far out of bounds it was not even funny. Of all the nocturnal quests that he had been on, tonight's was the farthest from school. As for the clue, it was more cryptic than ever before: *Idle persons shuffled here.* Jake turned the phrase over and over in his mind, trying to tease some meaning from it.

A glimmer of moonlight reflected off the canal. Three smackheads loitered under the railway bridge ahead, kicking a DID YOU WITNESS THIS CRIME? placard between them. Jake's heart pounded as he approached the men. His black sweater and black tracksuit bottoms were hardly conspicuous, but silence was just as important as camouflage. *Keep fast*, he breathed, *and light on your toes.*

The loiterers did not see Jake until he was among them, and no sooner had they registered his presence than he was gone again, under the railway bridge and up the side of the embankment, clawing his way through thick undergrowth and stinging nettles, breathing the sweet, cloying smells of wet vegetation and festering litter. There was some angry shouting from the towpath below him, and a brief, fumbling attempt at pursuit.

Jake vaulted a wooden fence, crossed the railway line, and scrambled through a hedge into a housing development. How many miles had he run? Four? Five? He sprinted southeast between brooding tower blocks and came out onto Hall Lane. The boarded-up windows of Mike's Carpets, Pet World, and Armley Bingo Hall glared at him as he passed. *Not far now.*

Latitude was bang on, so all he needed now was to continue east until he hit the right longitude. The lane was rising steeply, and the cold air made him wheeze. The flashing blue dot on his screen crept inexorably eastward. *Idle persons shuffled here. Idle persons shuffled here.*

1° 34' 40" west. *Perfect.*

Jake put his hands on his knees and gasped for breath. Then he straightened up and looked around. To his left was a high brick wall. To his right was a cemetery with tombstones leaning crazily in the moonlight. Jake shivered and checked his latitude. He was a fraction too far south, which meant that the thing he sought was not in the cemetery.

A loud voice in his left ear made him jump. "You are now standing at Leeds Prison, formerly known as Armley Jail. Leeds is a Category B prison, which once incarcerated the murderous cat burglar Charles Peace."

Jake took the earphone out of his left ear and slipped it into the money belt underneath his sweater. He had forgotten that HearPlanet was still running—it was a useful app, but annoying when it made you jump out of your skin.

So this was Leeds Prison, was it? He had seen it from the front, with its gleaming gates and slick visitors' center, but never from the back. Here an imposing brick wall stood fully fourteen feet high, topped with coils of barbed wire. Beyond the wire loomed the jagged crenellations of the jail itself, a Gothic horror against an inky sky.

Idle persons shuffled here. Jake groaned. It was an anagram! Shuffle the letters IDLE PERSONS and you got LEEDS PRISON. Griff must have lobbed the thimble over this very wall into the exercise yard beyond.

Jake and his mates in the dormitory had invented geothimble just a few weeks before, but it was fast becoming a craze, spreading to other houses and even other years. It was basically a high-tech version of the old-fashioned kids' game hunt the thimble. Boys took turns borrowing an item from someone else—a shoe, a chocolate bar, a penknife, whatever—and hiding it in a remote location. If the owner wanted his "thimble" back, he would have to get it himself, aided only by a GPS reference and a cryptic clue. Tonight's thimble, the object of Jake's quest, was a cardboard folder containing his geography project, which was due to be handed in the next day.

Thimbling a prison was cunning, just like Griff, but it was within the rules. Only last week Jake had slid Griff's watch into a mailbox on the other side of town, forcing Griff to wait until the early-morning collection and plead with a mailman. If this was Griff's revenge, so be it. Jake knew he would have to go for it. He had no intention of getting a failing grade this time.

Jake exited map mode and switched on his phone's flashlight to examine the barbed wire along the parapet. At one point there seemed to be a small gap between the bricks and the wire. With a bit of pushing and wriggling, perhaps he could get through. As for the fourteen-foot-high brick wall—well, that was also doable. He had something of a reputation among the thimblers.

Jake Knight's a legend. He can walk up walls.

Three years previously, Jake had watched his first YouTube wall run and had decided to master wall running himself. It was the urban cool and the challenge that attracted him, but also the philosophy. Walls were bad news. Walls were the enemy of exploration. Walls proclaimed: *Beyond this point you may not tread.* Wall running was about breaking those boundaries, mastering your environment—and yes, if truth be told, impressing your mates.

Jake stepped back and took three deep breaths, rehearsing the stunt in his mind. Then he ran toward the wall with short quick strides. His eyes were not on the wall itself but on the parapet above. *Don't focus on where you are* was his wall-run mantra. *Focus on where you want to be.* He gradually built up the power of his steps and jumped off his right foot. *I'm a spring,* he thought, *a tightly coiled spring.* He placed his left foot at chest level and launched himself upward, scrabbling with his hands to gain extra height. Another small kick from his right foot, and—*reach!*—he grabbed the parapet with both hands. *Made it.*

Jake dangled from the wall, gathering all his force for the final part of the move. Explosive energy was what was needed now. And—*liftoff!* He pulled with both arms and pushed with the balls of his feet. A second later the adventurer was lying along the top of the parapet, his quads and biceps burning, barbed wire tugging at his clothes, looking down into the well-lit exercise yard of Leeds Prison.

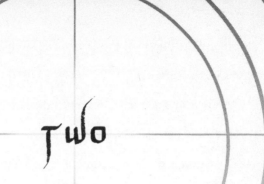

Two

The Chameleon stood in the shadows near the back of the crowd. He was eighteen years old and he wore a black cloak with a deep hood. He watched and listened as Sheikh Ahmed Abdullai Keita performed.

The sheikh's reputation had preceded him. All along the edge of the Sahara Desert, people spoke in awed whispers about the miracle man on the white stallion. Now he had arrived in the border town Mondoro, in the south of Mali, and he was doing what he did best. Miracles.

The sheikh sat on a straw mat in front of the chief's hut. He wore purple robes and a white prayer hat embroidered with sequins. Two braided locks of hair hung down, one on either side of his face. He had a short, pointed beard.

"People of Mondoro!" cried the sheikh. "The djinns of the

desert and the djinns of the air are here in power. Prepare yourselves for a visitation."

Ranged in a semicircle around the sheikh stood the villagers, their cheeks slack with wonder. In the last two hours the sheikh had sucked the malaria out of a sick man, made dozens of cola nuts disappear, and conjured a disembodied floating head out of thin air. Now he got up and ran through the crowd toward his magnificent stallion. "Behold!" he cried. "The djinns of the air are coming to bear me aloft on their warm, invisible hands."

With his arms stretched out on either side, the sheikh lifted into the air and hung there about two feet off the ground. The crowd behind him gasped. There was nervous laughter and cries of *"Allahu akbar!"*—"God is great!" Some cupped hands over their faces in pious supplication.

At the back of the crowd the Chameleon narrowed his eyes and drew his cloak around him more tightly. *It's an illusion,* he thought. *But how does he do it?*

The sheikh rose a little farther in the air and put his left foot into the nearside stirrup. Then he swung his right leg over the horse's back, sat down gently, and straightened his robe.

"Allahu akbar!" The cries rose on the night air.

The sheikh shook his head from side to side so that his locks swung like pendulums. Then he began to laugh—a deep, resonant laugh.

"The djinns of the desert mock you," he said. "You think you prosper, but tragedy is near."

"What tragedy?" The question rippled through the crowd.

"You look at the sky and grin, and you say to each other: *In a few short weeks the rains will begin and we will sow our seed.* Not so, fools! The djinns have hatched a plan. They will withhold the rain you long for. Not a drop of water will fall on Mondoro. Not a single stalk of millet will grow under the sun. Not a single peanut will form in the ground. From every eye salt water will flow."

"Is there nothing we can do?" asked one man. "Perhaps if we give the djinns more cola nuts—"

"Silence!" shouted the sheikh. "There is only one sacrifice that will appease the djinns of the desert. The sacrifice the djinns demand is this: fifty healthy young goats and fifty healthy young sheep. They must be taken to Senegal and sacrificed in the shallow waters of Lake Soum."

"Lake Soum?" said one. "I've never even heard of it!"

"Senegal is hundreds of miles away!" cried another.

"I will take pity on you," said the sheikh. "Have the animals ready by sunrise tomorrow. I will take them to Senegal and perform the sacrifice myself."

That night the women of Mondoro wept bitterly. *Sheikh Ahmed has demanded almost all the animals in the village,* they said. *What will be left for our children and our children's children? A handful of old, sick goats and nothing more.*

The men were adamant. *We are lucky,* they said, *that the sheikh warned us of the djinns' intention. It will hurt us to pay what the djinns demand, but we have no choice. We cannot risk a whole year's harvest. There is no such thing as an easy sacrifice.*

The men prevailed, and the next morning Sheikh Ahmed Abdullai Keita went on his way with fifty sheep and fifty goats. As soon as he was out of sight of the villagers, he entrusted the animals to one of his servants, ordering him to take the animals to a faraway market and sell them for hard cash.

Crouching behind a nearby acacia bush, the Chameleon observed the whole exchange. He tutted quietly and swore that he would teach this charlatan a lesson.

Three

I've heard of people breaking out of prison," said Mr. Joyce, the headmaster, peering over his half-moon glasses, "but why the devil would you break *into* one?"

"Sorry," said Jake. "It won't happen again."

"Correct," said Mr. Joyce, and he looked at Jake as he might have looked at a fruit fly in his compost bin.

Don't expel me, thought Jake. *Dad will go ape if I get expelled.*

"Knight by name, nocturnal by nature, what? How long have you been creeping out at night, Knight?"

"I don't go every night, sir. I go when it's my turn."

"When it's your turn!" Mr. Joyce puffed out his cheeks. With his big stomach and sagging jowls, he looked like a beached walrus. "While this school sleeps, Jake Knight slips out and paints the town red, provided it's his turn."

Jake was not sure what painting the town red meant, but he was fairly certain that geothimble did not count. And unless you counted school rules as law, it wasn't illegal, either. Geothimble was simply about conjuring adventure out of the tiresome work-eat-sleep fabric of boarding-school life. Plus it was a cool excuse for Jake and his mates to use the GPS function on their phones.

"Tell me, Knight," said Mr. Joyce, "what is the motto of this school?"

Jake furrowed his brow. "Who dares wins?" he guessed.

"I believe that is the motto of the Special Air Service," said the headmaster. "Though judging by your escapade last night, you might be more suited to the SAS than to any educational establishment."

"Thank you, sir."

"It was not a compliment," said the headmaster sternly. "Besides, you don't have nearly enough discipline for the military. You seem to have a rule allergy."

Either that or I just crave adventure, thought Jake. *What would Mr. Joyce say about Lawrence of Arabia or Captain Cook? Would he diagnose them with rule allergy?*

"The school motto, Knight, is this: *Ad astra per aspera.* Through adversity to the stars."

"Yes, sir."

"Adversity, Knight. Trials. Difficulties. Have you ever experienced adversity?"

"I don't know, sir."

"How much did your phone cost?"

None of your business, thought Jake. "Three hundred pounds, sir," he said.

"Three *hundred* pounds. And how old are you?"

"Fifteen, sir."

"*Fifteen!* It's no wonder you've gone off the rails, Knight. You've never known adversity."

Hadn't he? Here he was, cooped up in a stuffy English boarding school, while his parents and his sister lived their African adventure under an ever-smiling sun. He hadn't asked to go to boarding school. The decision, as always, had been made for him.

The headmaster was warming to the adversity theme. "Have you ever been hungry or thirsty, Knight? Have you ever been in need? Have you ever had to choose between food and medicine?"

"No, sir," said Jake.

"Have you ever faced up to a metaphorical giant armed with only a metaphorical sling and five small stones?"

"No, sir."

"Of course you haven't. You are the son of a British ambassador. You bask in entitlement. You click your fingers and the stars drop out of the sky into your lap. You lack for nothing."

Hang on, thought Jake. *Griff may be like that, but not me. I could click my fingers all day and get nothing but blistered fingertips. It took me a whole summer of freelance web design to buy that phone. I earned it.*

"Sorry, sir" was all he said.

The door opened and Jake's housemaster, Mr. Blake, shuffled in. Mr. Blake greeted the headmaster and nodded mournfully at Jake.

Don't tell me I'm expelled, thought Jake again.

"I asked Mr. Blake to be present," said the headmaster, "because I have the unpleasant duty to inform you that you will be leaving us."

I'm dead, thought Jake.

"I'm going to nip this geothimble in the bud," said Mr. Joyce, "and in doing so, I'm going to make an example of you, Knight. You have too much technology and too little moral fiber. As of this moment you are suspended."

Mr. Blake flinched and gazed at Jake with mournful eyes, as if his pupil had just been voted off some reality TV show.

"How long for, sir?"

"For the rest of term."

Jake blew out his cheeks. He was so relieved, he felt like leaping up onto the headmaster's desk and dancing a fandango. He would miss six weeks of school, but that was all.

"We will be informing your parents, of course," said the headmaster, "so that they can make the necessary arrangements. I imagine you will be flying out to Upper Volta to join them, what?"

Upper Volta? Mr. Joyce was forty years out of date. The tiny West African country was no longer a French colony, and it was certainly no longer called Upper Volta. Today it was an independent state, Burkina Faso, home to sixteen million people including Mum, Dad, and his sister, Kirsty, called Kas. Jake looked out of the window and thought of Africa. He would not be sorry to see the back of Waltham College. Leeds was no place for an adventurer.

"I will phone your father later this morning," the headmaster was saying. "As for you, Knight, you will pack your belongings and leave Waltham College by sundown tomorrow. The secretary will email you any essential schoolwork in due course. Do your assignments, reform your character, and perhaps we will be seeing you in the summer term."

"Yes, sir." Jake stood up to go.

"Just one more thing, Knight." The headmaster gazed over his spectacles, small eyes shining in his flabby face. "How the devil did you climb a sheer wall more than twice your height?"

Four

Mesdames et messieurs, we have arrived at Ouagadougou International Airport. The time is nine fifteen p.m.,
and the temperature is thirty-two degrees centigrade."

According to Jake's GPS, Ouagadougou was due south of
Leeds. But the shared longitude was where any similarity ended.
Here in Burkina Faso the sun shone from dawn till dusk and life
was one long adventure.

Jake hid his phone in a sock and shoved it into a dark corner
of his carryon bag. Wouldn't want to be charged import duty on
something that wasn't even brand-new. He made his way off the
plane in a heat-induced daze, down the steps two at a time, on
and off a crowded shuttle bus, through the various checkpoints—
passport, immunization papers, visa—around a dilapidated luggage carousel, past four nimble-fingered customs officers—*Don't*

look in the sock—and out into the airport forecourt. Taxi drivers pressed around him, eager for custom.

It felt good to be back in Burkina Faso, as if a heavy weight had been lifted off his shoulders. This was Jake's fifth visit to the country, and it looked like it would be the longest ever: half the spring term and all of the Easter holidays—ten whole weeks of freedom. Here he could truly be himself, seizing each day as it came with no thought for the next. Here his life would not be regulated by clanging bells and finger-wagging teachers. In Africa time did not matter. Everyone just went with the flow.

"You are two hours late!" bayed a no-nonsense English voice, and the gaggle of taxi drivers parted to let Jake's father through. He looked the same as usual: tall, angular, and harassed. Worry lines furrowed his brow, and his close-cropped beard glistened with sweat.

"Hello, Dad," said Jake.

"Hello indeed. What's this blinking geothimble?"

Jake had not expected his father to have calmed down much since they'd talked on the phone.

"It's basically a techno version of hunt the thimble," he said. "Gran taught me that."

"Did she indeed? And I suppose Gran also taught you how to be a ne'er-do-well and how to break into prisons and how to get yourself booted out of one of the finest schools in England. Now follow me, quickly."

"Did you come on the motorcycle?" asked Jake, half running to keep up.

"Yes."

They weaved through the jostling crowd and out into a floodlit parking lot. There, gleaming on its stand, stood his father's BMW Dakar tour bike. With its sleek curves and broad handlebars, it looked more like a prize bull than a motorcycle.

They tied the bags to the back of the Dakar and got on. "Do you want to know what really infuriates me in all of this?" asked Mr. Knight, pulling on his leather gloves. "The thing that appalls me to the core of my being?"

"Go on," said Jake.

"It's the fact that I heard the news about your suspension from your sister a full two hours before Mr. Joyce phoned and four hours before you called. And how did Kirsty know you'd been suspended? Where had she happened upon this toothsome morsel of news?"

Oops, thought Jake.

"Twitter!" exploded the ambassador, and he gave the start pedal a ferocious kick.

The motorcycle burst into life with a deep, throaty roar. Biking was Mr. Knight's hobby, although the word "hobby" hardly did justice to the fervent passion that he bestowed on his BMW Dakar.

"Have you made any more modifications to the bike?" asked Jake.

"Don't try to change the subject!" snapped Mr. Knight, pulling out onto the main road. "As a matter of fact, I have," he added. "You can't see it from where you are, but I've fitted a bash plate all along the underside, with a hidden chamber in it."

"What's in the hidden chamber?"

"You name it, it's in there. Tool kit, spare parts, ration pack, distress flares, glow sticks, first-aid kit, survival blanket, vitamin C, salt, water purification tablets, and six liters of water."

"Cool."

"Yes, the whole chamber is insulated to protect it from engine heat. I managed to find some desert rally tires, too. They're filled with race mousse instead of air, so they don't deflate even if they get punctured."

"Nice."

"Then I reinforced the subframe, doubled the size of the fuel tank, fitted stronger bearings in the gearbox, replaced the suspension shocks, and tuned the engine for maximum performance—listen!"

Ambassador Knight pulled out into the fast lane and gunned the throttle. Jake's knuckles whitened on the chrome handgrips, and he had to tense his neck to stop his head from flying off. There was no denying it: this bike was a demon.

As they shot through the dark streets of Ouagadougou, Jake looked around him. He had always been here during school holidays, and he had loved it every time. Engine oil, charcoal, and warm earth in his nostrils, Bob Marley in his ears, warm "Ouaga" air in his lungs. Magic.

They were out of the city center now and zooming hell-for-leather along Avenue Charles de Gaulle. Past the president's palace, with its whitewashed walls and its platoon of elite *gendarmes* always on patrol. Past the university, with its dingy bars and photocopy booths. Past the night market with its dimly lit fruit stalls and its cabinets of scrawny, ever-rotating chickens.

Just before the Save the Children office, Jake's father closed the throttle and veered deftly into a side street. This was Zone du Bois, the leafiest and richest district in Ouagadougou. A minute later they arrived on Embassy Row and pulled up outside the gates of the British embassy.

Saalu, the night guard, shook Jake's hand and smiled his gap-toothed smile. "*Bonsoir*, Jake," he said.

"*Ça va*, Saalu?" said Jake. Lots of African languages were spoken in Burkina Faso, but the official language was French. Jake was nearly fluent. French was his best subject at school, and he had practiced it with increasing success on each of his African visits.

The night guard used a mirror on a long stick to examine the underside of the bike, checking for explosive devices. Then he stepped aside and slid open the heavy metal gates. The BMW prowled up the gravel path and stopped under a thatched gazebo. On one side was the embassy, on the other the family home. Around the back were Mum's beehives and a small swimming pool. If bikes were Dad's passion, bees were Mum's. She was crazy about them.

Kas came running out and threw her arms around Jake. She was taller than he remembered, and was wearing black eye makeup.

"No!" cried Jake. "Don't tell me my little sis has gone emo."

"Hello," replied Kas. "How's life in the Bradford-Leeds criminal underworld?"

"Thirteen is too young for black eye makeup."

"Fifteen is too young for prison breaking."

"Where's Mum?"

"Round the back, messing with her precious bees. She'll be here in a minute."

"I can't believe you told Dad about me getting suspended."

"Seemed like the right thing to do. How come you managed to get into the prison but not out?"

"I tried loads of times, but there was this bear of an overhang on the inside of the wall. I couldn't get any grip at all."

"Bizarre. Anyone would think they had designed the prison to stop people from escaping." Kas did an elaborate curtsey before prattling on. "If I were you, I wouldn't play any geek-o-thimble here in Ouaga, Jake. Most of the walls are topped with broken glass."

Jake shrugged. "I'm not scared of a bit of glass," he said.

"Well, just be careful," said Kas. "And if you ever use my hair straighteners as a thimble, I'll drown you in the swimming pool."

Jake laughed. It was good to see Kas again. And there was definitely no need for geothimble here in Africa. Geothimble was about staving off boredom, and here he never got bored. Here in Africa stuff happened.

FIVE

The Chameleon sat in the shade of a baobab tree within sight of the Petagoli well. He had been waiting since sunrise, and so far there was no sign of the sheikh and his traveling party. Rumor had it that the sheikh crossed the border into Burkina Faso two days earlier and was heading for Djibo, ancient seat of the Jelgooji kings. He should be passing this way either today or tomorrow.

The Chameleon was wearing a loose cotton garment and conical hat, his shepherding disguise. He carried a crooked staff and had a water bottle slung over his shoulder.

Shortly after midafternoon prayers, his patience was rewarded. A white stallion loped into view, its golden bridle glinting in the sun. Atop the horse sat the familiar figure of the sheikh, resplendent in his purple robes and white prayer hat. His minstrel was mounted on a second horse, and five servants followed on foot.

The Chameleon ran to the well, lowered the bucket, and flicked the rope deftly to fill the bucket with water. The sheikh's traveling party drew level with the well and stopped.

"Sheikh Ahmed Abdullai Keita of Senegal!" cried the minstrel. "Beloved of God, Friend of Djinns, Pillar of Righteousness!"

The Chameleon threw himself face-down on the ground in front of the stallion. "I am only a simple shepherd boy," he said, "but I know the name Sheikh Ahmed Abdullai Keita. The reputation of Sheikh Ahmed wafts before him like the fragrance of heaven. Welcome to Burkina Faso, your excellency. In the name of Allah, allow me to water your horses."

"Be quick about it," snapped the sheikh. "I must be in Djibo before nightfall."

"Forgive my impudence," said the Chameleon, "but what you propose is quite impossible, unless your horses have wings, which I do not discount."

"I was told we were close."

"Close!" The Chameleon chuckled as if at a good joke. "I was born here and I know every tree in the province. From here to Djibo is one hundred ghalva as the herder bird flies, and not one ghalva less."

The sheikh turned to his navigator-minstrel and began to remonstrate with him. The minstrel shrugged and held up his hands, bewildered by this new information.

The Chameleon gave the horses water and patted their noses as they drank. So far the encounter was going according to plan.

After an urgent conference with his minstrel, Sheikh Ahmed summoned the shepherd boy. "Tell me, boy," he said. "Who is the emir in these parts?"

"My father is the emir," said the Chameleon, "and I beg you to say no more, for I understand already what you need. My father is a hospitable man. He is away on business at present, but my brothers and I would be honored to welcome you in his stead. You may stay at our humble settlement for as long as you wish."

SIX

The day after Jake's arrival, the Knight family was invited to a banquet at the Hotel Libya—a celebration of ten years since commercial gold mining had started in the north of Burkina Faso. Jake wore a jacket and one of his dad's ties. Kas wore a black dress, her skull-bow necklace, and even more eyeliner than usual.

"It's way more than ten years since those gold mines started," said Kas in the car on the way to the hotel. "Africans have been mining gold there for hundreds of years."

"So what?" said Jake.

"So what we're actually celebrating tonight is *not* ten years since the gold mines started, but ten years since a foreign mining company bought those mines from the government and drove hundreds of indigenous workers off their ancestral land."

"You didn't have to come, you know," snapped Mrs. Knight.

"I wanted to," said Kirsty, craning her neck to smooth her already-smooth hair in the rearview mirror. "It's an excuse to get dolled up, innit?"

Sometimes Jake found it hard to tell whether or not his sister was being sarcastic.

They arrived at the Hotel Libya, parked the car, and went inside. The furnishings in the banqueting hall were eye-wateringly lavish: gold chandeliers, crisp white table linen, gold vases crammed with fire orchids, gold candlesticks—even the knives and forks were gold. Jake put his phone on video mode and stood at the doorway filming the splendid panorama.

"Solid gold," whispered Jake's mum, weighing a fork in her hand.

Kas was unimpressed. "Don't the gold barons know how many people are starving in this city? I guess they've shoved their heads so far down their own mines that they—" She broke off quickly when she saw her father's expression.

"Any more rants from you, Kirsty, and I will ground you for a month, is that clear?"

"Yes, Dad," said Kas, but she rolled her eyes as she turned away.

They soon found their names on the seating plan. Jake had Kas on one side of him and his mum on the other. Mr. Knight was farther up the table, with the mine directors. Jake held his phone under the table, uploaded the gold banquet video to Facebook, and tweeted a link to it with the simple caption *Nice*.

A shadow fell across the table. A large uniformed man was taking his place opposite Jake.

"Do you know who that is?" said Jake's mum in a sibilant whisper. "It's *Haut Commissaire* François Beogo, commissioner of police for the whole country."

The commissioner made a gun shape with his hand and grinned at Kas. "Your necklace or your life," he hissed in English.

"I'll keep the necklace," said Kas. "Life is overrated."

"Kirsty, don't be morbid," said Mrs. Knight. "Commissioner, you don't have to speak English. Jake and Kirsty speak fluent French."

Kas snorted. "Or in Jake's case, fluent French with a Yorkshire accent."

"Hey!" said Jake, and the commissioner laughed.

"I am sure you both speak excellent French," he said, "but let us speak in English tonight. I need the practice."

The appetizer arrived—a seafood platter of Atlantic salmon,

whitebait, meaty shrimp, and lemon segments. Mrs. Knight turned to the man on her right and began to tell him about the agony and ecstasy of beekeeping, leaving Jake and Kirsty free to talk to the police commissioner. With his twinkling eyes and ready laugh, he was a very likeable man.

"Tell me, Jake," said Commissioner Beogo, "what do you think of our country?"

"I like it," said Jake. "Reggae everywhere you go, guavas and watermelons everywhere you look, table football on every street corner. It's the best country in the world."

"Or at least in the top twenty," said Kas.

"I wish I could see our country through your eyes," said Beogo, "but my job keeps me focused on the dark underbelly of society. The underground gangs, the drug runners, the warlords. It warps your outlook, Jake."

"Is there a lot of crime?"

"So much, it would make your hair stand on end. I could tell you true crime stories that would make your skeleton wobble like *sagabo*."

Jake laughed at the image. *Sagabo* was a local dish, a maize dumpling that quivered when you lifted it to your mouth. "Go on, then," he said. "Let's hear a few."

The main course arrived—a quarter duck so tender that it

fell off the bone. As he ate, the police commissioner told stories about Burkina Faso's most notorious highwaymen, bandits, and outlaws. Jake and Kas listened agog, and they kept saying "cool" until they realized how much it annoyed him.

"Outlaws are a long way from being cool," snapped Beogo. "Outlaws are thieves and murderers, and there is not a speck of cool in any of them. Just last month an ambulance belonging to the Aribinda Hospital of Hope was hijacked in the bush by two highwaymen. An ambulance, I tell you, taking a sick old woman to the hospital!"

"What happened?" asked Jake.

"They drove the ambulance across the border into Mali and sold it as a cattle truck."

"What about the old woman?"

"We found her bones in a termite mound by the side of the road, ten miles out of Aribinda."

"Eeuw," said Kas. "So what do you do if you catch an outlaw?"

"If he is lucky," said Beogo, "we try him in a court of law."

"And if he is unlucky?"

The police commissioner held up his gold knife and drew it theatrically across his own throat.

"Are there outlaws here in Ouagadougou?" Kas wanted to know.

"Not many. Most of them operate in the desert, a couple hundred miles north of here."

"Dad has done some biking up there," said Jake. "It sounds amazing."

"It is beautiful," agreed the police commissioner, "but dangerous. My people say that the deserts of the north are a battlefield for angels and demons. As for the *desserts* of the south," he added drily, looking at the chocolate tortes that were being brought to the tables, "they are an altogether different battlefield."

Jake could not help gaping at the desserts. Each minitorte was smothered in warm chocolate fudge sauce and decorated lavishly with gold leaf.

"Is that what I think it is?" asked Kas.

"Genuine twenty-four-carat gold," said Mrs. Knight, reading off the menu. "Don't worry, Kirsty, it's perfectly edible."

"Great," said Kas. "That's all right, then."

Mrs. Knight missed the sarcasm. She picked up a golden spoon, took a scoop of gold leaf and chocolate, and popped it into her mouth.

"Did anyone see that woman in the hotel parking lot tonight?" asked Kas.

"Mmmm." Mrs. Knight was loving the torte. "What did you say, darling?"

"A woman in the parking lot," said Kas. "She was carrying two babies in a sling—one on her back and one on her front. She was holding out her hands, begging for small change, and one of her hands was sort of curled up."

"Leprosy," said the police commissioner.

"It's a common enough sight," said Mrs. Knight. "The world is very hard on some people."

"Hard for us, too, of course," said Kas, her voice cracking, "what with all this bleedin' gold to digest."

"Kirsty, don't swear."

"Do you think our friend in the parking lot will swear when I tell her we've spent the whole evening stuffing ourselves with gold?"

"Kirsty Knight, pipe down. You're being completely over the top."

"I need air." Kas pushed back her chair, stood up, and walked out.

The police commissioner picked up a gold-colored napkin and wiped his mouth slowly, evidently embarrassed by the confrontation. Jake glanced along the table and saw his father scowling. Kas would have hell to pay later.

Jake finished his torte in silence. He did not like the thought of his sister's dessert going to waste, so he ate that as well. Then, holding his phone under the table, he touch-typed a tweet: Eatin gold & lovin it.

"You'd better go and find Kirsty," said Mrs. Knight. "Tell her to come back inside this minute."

Jake's mission turned out to be harder than it sounded. He expected to find Kas shuffling moodily around the parking lot or perched on the hood of the family car, but she was nowhere to be seen.

He wandered over to the east wing of the hotel, where the swimming pool was. It was deserted, apart from a bored-looking waiter over by the lounge chairs.

"*Bonsoir!*" the waiter called to Jake. "If you want to swim after dark, you must be accompanied by an adult."

"I don't want to swim," said Jake. "I'm looking for my sister."

"What does she look like?"

"White skin, black makeup, black hair," Jake said, pointing at his shoulder to indicate the length.

The waiter nodded. "Round the back."

Jake followed his directions to the back of the hotel. As his eyes adjusted to the darkness, he made out the shapes of four big black trash containers. They exuded a foul smell, which made Jake want to retch.

"Did you eat the gold?" The voice in the shadows down at Jake's feet made him jump. It was Kas, crouching on a wooden crate next to one of the bins.

"Of course," said Jake.

"I hope you choke on it." It was too dark to see Kas's eyes, but he could tell by her voice that she had been crying.

"Mum told me to find you," said Jake. "She says to come back in straightaway."

"Too bad. I'm waiting for someone."

"Who?"

"That woman with the withered hand."

"She was in the parking lot," said Jake.

"Well, she's not anymore. That waiter by the pool told me she sometimes comes round here to forage for food."

"Why do you want to see her?"

"To give her this."

Jake squinted down at the object in his sister's hand—a solid-gold fork from the banqueting hall. "You can't do that," he heard himself say. "That's stealing."

"Stealing from the rich to give to the poor," said Kas. "It's Robin Hood, innit?"

"It's still stealing," said Jake, taking the fork from her hand.

"Hypocrite," said Kas. "Talking of which, can you believe Mum called *me* OTT? That banquet was the most over-the-top thing I've ever seen in my life."

Jake heard the purr of a car engine and he looked up, shielding his eyes against the sudden glare of headlights. It was a delivery van, an orange and yellow Nissan with JUMBO written across it in huge letters. Jake remembered these vans from his previous visits to Burkina Faso. They were everywhere in Ouagadougou, zooming around the city, selling Jumbo chicken-stock cubes to small traders.

The door of the van opened and a man got out, leaving the engine running. He went around to the back of the van, opened the double doors, and started over to where Jake and Kirsty were. He wore a baseball cap and sunglasses.

"Bonsoir," said the man. "I have a pickup to make."

"Nothing to do with us," muttered Kas.

"Au contraire," said the man, and he grabbed her by the wrists.

seven

"**Hey!**" shouted Jake. "Get off her!"

The man pushed him over with one hard shove in the chest. As he fell, Jake's head hit the corner of a trash container, fracturing his world into a kaleidoscope of color. He shook his head to clear his vision and saw his sister's assailant silhouetted in the headlights. He was walking back to the van with Kas slung over his shoulder like a sack of meal.

Jake sprang to his feet and chased after the stranger, closing his fist around the only weapon he had to hand, the golden fork. He caught up with him right by the doors of the delivery van and plunged the fork into the back of the man's thigh. The kidnapper yelped and staggered and dropped his hostage.

"Come on!" Jake grabbed his sister's hand and pulled her up. Side by side they ran along the back of the hotel. From the darkness behind them he heard the slam of a van door and a frenzy of revving, but they did not look back. They burst out of the alleyway and sprinted alongside the swimming pool, heading for the glittering lights of the hotel lobby.

The poolside waiter was perched on one of the lounge chairs, chin in hands, but he jumped to his feet when he saw Jake and Kas. *"Calmez-vous!"* he cried, stepping out into their path. "Slow down! No running by the pool!"

"Get out of the way!" shouted Jake. "Someone's after us!"

As if to confirm his words, the Nissan burst through the shrubbery at the other end of the pool and careered toward them, plowing through chairs, umbrellas, and plastic coffee tables.

The waiter bent down and picked up a large net used for clearing leaves out of the swimming pool. As Jake and Kas ran past him, he swung the pole in a wide arc and brought the net down over their heads, trapping them both in its mesh. Jake felt a sharp pain in his left temple as his sister's head collided with his own.

They're working together, thought Jake. *The delivery man and the waiter. They're both in on this thing, whatever it is.* Jake's vision narrowed suddenly, and he was very aware of his own breathing, fast and loud.

The van screeched to a stop right behind them, and Jake and Kas were dragged toward it. Jake caught a whiff of cheap after-shave as the waiter bundled them into the back. Doors slammed, and the vehicle moved off fast, its wheels spinning on the pool-side tiles.

"Kirsty, are you all right?" said Jake.

"My head hurts," sobbed Kirsty.

So did Jake's. He could hardly think straight, it hurt so much. He took his phone out, switched on the flashlight function, and had a look around. They were in the van's storage area, separated from the driver's cab by a thick wooden partition. Piled up against the partition were about forty huge wooden crates of stock cubes. The smell was overpowering.

"Help!" Jake lashed out at the sides of the van with his fists and feet. "We're being kidnapped!"

"Help!" echoed Kirsty. "Somebody, please, help us!"

Immediately the van's loudspeaker crackled into life. Every Jumbo advertising van had a triangular speaker mounted on top, useful for blaring out local dance music and stock-cube info-mercials. Jake and Kirsty's banging and shouting were soon drowned out by an earsplitting techno beat.

"*Jumbo poulet, Jumbo poulet!*" thundered a man's voice on the loudspeaker.

"Enrichi en vitamine A!" sang a backup group.

"Jumbo-Jumbo!"

"Poulet-poulet!"

"Enrichi en vitamine A!"

Jake and Kas's desperate yells resounded within the van, but passersby outside would be hearing only Jumbo music. This was a perfect kidnap vehicle, proclaiming chicken-flavored innocence down every byway.

"Ring my phone," said Kas. "It's in Mum's handbag."

The signal inside the van was faint—only one bar—but it was enough. After a couple of rings, Mrs. Knight answered. "Jake," she said, "have you found Kirsty? Tell her to come back this minute."

"Mum, we've been kidnapped."

"I can't hear a word you're saying, Jake. Step away from the speakers."

"We're in a van, Mum. We're being abducted."

"What?"

"Abducted," said Jake. "Kidnapped."

"No!" The word was somewhere between a shriek and a sob.

"We were round the back of the hotel and this man came for us. We're in a Jumbo van. Orange and yellow."

"You're with Kas?"

"Yes."

"Are you hurt?" Mrs. Knight was properly crying now.

"He banged our heads together. I'm nearly out of battery, Mum."

"We'll call you back, Jake. Everything will be all right, do you hear?"

Jake hung up. The van was going faster now, and the surface of the road was smoother, as if they had turned out of the hotel parking lot onto a main road. Every moment was taking them farther away from their parents.

"What's happening?" asked Kas.

"They're going to call us back."

"Make sure your phone's on Mosquito."

The Mosquito was the most downloaded ringtone of the decade. It was the ultimate in subversive classroom communication, a ringtone exploiting the fact that some frequencies of sound are audible only to under-twenties. After a few moments of silence the phone began to whine. Jake handed his sister an earphone and kept one for himself.

"Hello," said Kas.

"Hello, princess." This time it was their father's voice, cool and level. "How is your head?"

"It hurts."

"Your mother and I love you both very much. You know that. But right now we have to master our emotions."

"I'm scared, Dad."

"Of course you are. But the sooner you regain your composure, the better off you will be. There are two of you, so you can help each other with that. Breathe together, really long deep breaths. Are you breathing?"

"Yes."

"We're going to get you back."

"I know."

"Good girl. Is your brother there?"

"Yes," said Jake.

"This is going to turn out all right, son. Tell me, how many men were there?"

"Two."

"African?"

"Yes."

"French speaking?"

"Yes."

"Turbans?"

"No."

"Listen carefully, both of you. I've done training on this sort of thing, and I'm going to give you some important advice. You must cooperate with these people, whoever they are. Don't make them angry. Don't whine. And Kas, don't be sarcastic."

"All right."

"Don't resist them in any way. And whatever you do, don't look them in the eyes. They will interpret that as a challenge."

Jake felt a convulsion in his throat and put his hand over his mouth. *Adventurers don't cry,* he told himself.

"You've done really well so far," continued Mr. Knight. "The most dangerous part of any abduction is the first few minutes. That's when kidnappers are most stressed out and most likely to be violent. What else do you remember about them?"

"Not much."

"Come on, son. The more information we can give to the police, the sooner they can find you."

"The driver is wearing a black T-shirt, black trousers, baseball cap, and sunglasses—"

"*Sunglasses?* At night?"

"Yes. The other one is dressed as a waiter. Short-sleeved white shirt, bow tie, black trousers."

"He had a tattoo," said Kirsty.

"A tattoo? Well done, princess! Whereabouts?"

"On his arm. A spider in a web."

"Did either of them h—" Mr. Knight broke off suddenly, then tried again. "Did either of them have a gun?"

"Didn't see one," said Kas.

"Can you describe the van?"

"Orange and yellow Nissan. Just a normal Jumbo publicity van."

"License plate?"

"Don't know."

"Do you have any idea where you are?"

"We're all boxed in," said Jake, "so I can't get a proper GPS fix. All I have is a basic cell tower ID."

"How accurate is that?"

"In the city, it gives a position to within about three hundred meters."

"Can you send it to me?"

"I can do better than that. I can set my phone to publish the cell tower ID to Twitter every thirty seconds."

"How do I access it?"

"Get hold of Griff Keating," said Jake. "He's a year ahead of me at school. He knows all about positioning."

"I'll give him a call," said Mr. Knight. "There's one more thing I want you both to promise me. Don't try to escape."

"Why not?"

"It's too dangerous. When a hostage gets injured or killed, it's usually the result of some harebrained escape attempt. Just stay where you are, keep your phone out of sight, and breathe nice and slow."

"Okay."

"Look after each other. Try to keep your spirits up. You'll be home before you know it. I'm going to talk to Commissioner Beogo and then phone the Foreign Office. I'll ring you soon." Mr. Knight sobbed and tried to disguise it as a cough. Then the line went dead.

Jake pulled off his tie and crouched next to Kas in the darkness, breathing in the musty smell of fear and chicken-stock cubes. *I was hoping for adventure,* thought Jake, *but this is not what I had in mind.*

eight

The Chameleon was an excellent host. He gave Sheikh Ahmed Abdullai the place of honor in the banqueting tent, a reclining wicker chair piled high with leather cushions. On a table at the sheikh's right hand was arrayed a dazzling variety of meat and drink: calabashes of peanuts and chickpeas, skewers of succulent roasted goat, sweet red onions, sprigs of rosemary, and a mound of rice drenched in palm oil. There were soft black dates from the slopes of Tamanrasset and a constant flow of tea laced with fresh mint and ginger.

The tent was warm and full of laughter. As the constellation Orion rose in the night sky, a trio of minstrels strummed on their three-stringed lutes, reciting for their guest the heroic ballad of Askia Muhammad. The sheikh congratulated himself on his good fortune to have been welcomed so warmly in this desert paradise. He grinned and consumed and let the music wash over him, entirely drunk with pleasure.

"More goat for his holiness," cried the Chameleon, clicking his fingers at the serving boys. "And bring a goblet of Mariama's mango wine. *Ko weedu heewi fu, na yidi hebbiteede.* Even if a lake is full, it can always take some more!"

The sheikh mumbled his thanks and slumped farther down into his nest of cushions. He accepted two more skewers of goat and a large clay goblet brimming with mango wine. He was beginning to feel sleepy.

"I must leave you for a few moments, Sheikh Ahmed," murmured the Chameleon. "Make yourself at home."

He slipped out into the moist night air and walked to the Needle Hut, where Paaté the tailor was hard at work. Paaté was eighteen, the same age as the Chameleon, and they were the best of friends.

"*Salaam aleykum,* Paaté," said the Chameleon, clapping his friend on the back. "How is my robe coming along?"

"*Aleykum asalaam,*" said Paaté. "I'm sewing on the last sequins now."

"And the wig?"

"Already done." Paaté pointed to a row of upturned calabashes on a nearby workbench, one of which wore a fine black wig with two braided locks of hair dangling down in front. "Do you think it looks like him?"

"It's perfect," said the Chameleon. "And what about my magic shoes?"

"Over there," said Paaté, pointing at a pair of camel-skin moccasins in the corner of the hut.

"And my false stomach?"

"Make it yourself," said Paaté. "Why should I do all the work?"

"Because you do it so well."

"And another thing," said Paaté. "Why do we have to be nice to that hateful man for two whole days and waste perfectly good food on him?"

The Chameleon raised his eyebrows. "What would you have me do?"

"What we always do to villains. Teach him a lesson."

"And what of the other men in his traveling party? The minstrel and the five servants. Should they also be taught a lesson?"

"Certainly they should. If they follow him, they must be as wicked as he is."

"Wicked men are very rare," said the Chameleon. "Unimaginative men are far more common. Talk to them, Paaté. Help them to see that they have a choice."

Paaté frowned. "So I stay here and preach to five unwashed servants and an irritating minstrel, while you go gallivanting around the province with your magic shoes."

The Chameleon grinned and clicked his heels together. "Precisely," he said. "The grain merchants of Djibo are about to get the shock of their lives."

ηιηe

Ever heard of Mungo Park?" asked Jake.

"No," said Kas. "Why?"

"Famous explorer. Went on two long journeys, mapping the river Niger all the way to its source. Wrote a book about his adventures, *Travels in the Interior of Africa*. I was reading it on the plane."

"And you're telling me this because . . . ?"

"Because he got kidnapped, too, at one point. He was taken prisoner by a wicked Moor in Hausaland, but after a month he managed to escape."

"You're loving this little adventure of ours, aren't you?" said Kas.

"No."

"Yes, you are. You're thinking about how this is going to

look to your mates back home. Big Mungo Jake, intrepid African explorer, kidnapped in Ouagadougou by a man with a spider tattoo. Well, just you wait until Mr. Spider Tattoo gets nasty and—"

"All right, keep your hair on. I only mentioned Mungo Park because Dad told us to keep our spirits up. And if you think I'm enjoying any of this, then you've got even less brain than—"

The Mosquito whined suddenly, making them jump. Jake put his earphones in.

"Jake." It was his father's voice. "How are you bearing up?"

"Not bad," said Jake. "We're still in the van."

"How's that slow breathing going?"

"Fine. Did you speak to Griff?"

"Yes. He's a bright lad, isn't he? He combined your Twitter feed with a map of Burkina Faso, so we can follow your progress in real time. You are still heading north away from Ouagadougou. There is only one road north, and that's the road that leads to Kongoussi and Djibo."

"Good," said Jake. "They know which road we're on," he whispered to Kas.

"Commissioner Beogo has scrambled four police vehicles," continued Mr. Knight. "Two from Ouagadougou and two from Kongoussi. The cars will converge on your position within the next half hour. Is there anything else in the back of the van with you?"

"Stock-cube crates," said Jake. "Loads of them."

"Capital," said Mr. Knight. "Arrange them all around you as best you can. When the police catch up with the van, there may be some shooting. It's probably nothing to worry about. Beogo will tell his men to fire only at the driver's cab."

"Do you know who the kidnappers are?"

"Maybe." Jake heard the hesitation in his father's voice. "Look, I don't want to scare you, but you might as well know. Beogo says there is a man called Yakuuba Sor who has a tattoo exactly like the one Kirsty described. He leads a gang of outlaws called the Friends of the Poor, and they live in the desert in the far north of Burkina Faso."

Yakuuba Sor, thought Jake. *Even the name sounds evil.* "What does Sor want?"

"He has not yet contacted us with his demands. But Commissioner Beogo seems to believe that the Friends of the Poor are an African branch of . . ." Mr. Knight hesitated.

"An African branch of what?"

"It's probably nothing," said Mr. Knight. "Like I said, I don't want to scare you."

"A branch of what?" repeated Jake.

"You're breaking up," said his father. "I think I'm losing you."

"It's just money, isn't it? All they want is money, right, Dad?"

The phone crackled and went dead.

"What's wrong?" asked Kas.

"I lost him," said Jake. He looked down at his phone. There was no signal.

"What did he say?"

"He said we should hide in the middle of these crates. Make a sort of barricade in case there's any shooting."

"Shooting!"

"Shooting is good, Kas. Shooting means it's almost over. The police know exactly where we are and they're coming for us. They've got two police cars coming from the north and two police cars from the south, and they're going to make themselves a kidnapper sandwich."

But Jake spoke with more confidence than he felt. With no phone signal, they could no longer relay their position to Dad. The police operation would work only if the kidnap vehicle stayed on the same road and did not make any sudden changes of direction.

"Does Dad know who's behind all this?" asked Kas.

To tell or not to tell, thought Jake. At the banquet Kas had enjoyed Beogo's stories about black-hearted outlaws in the deserts of the north, but only because there seemed little chance of meeting one. He put a hand on his sister's arm. "They're not sure," he said. "Come on, let's make that barricade."

Jake switched on the flashlight and they started arranging the crates in a protective circle, five crates high and two crates deep. It felt good to be doing something constructive at last.

"Cute," said Kas, surveying their handiwork. "It's like those dens we used to make when we were little."

Suddenly the van swung hard to the left, careering off the smooth macadam onto what felt like a rough dirt track. With no seats to cushion the impact, every rut and hole made Jake and Kas wince or cry out. Then came the big one, the mother and father of all potholes. The van's undercarriage slammed into the edge of the hole with a sickening crunch.

"Take cover!" shouted Jake, wrapping his arms around his head as the packing-crate walls shivered and collapsed. His head was protected, but the rest of him took a real battering. Kas, too, by the sound of it.

Jake rubbed his elbow and felt the sticky warmth of blood.

"We've gone off-road, haven't we?" said Kas.

"Yes."

"That's it, then. There's no way the police can find us now."

"You never know," said Jake. "They might see the tire tracks."

"Or they might not. Anyway, I need the toilet."

"Try not to think about it."

They sat in silence, bracing themselves against the sides of the van as it juddered over a series of bone-rattling ruts and dips.

"I wonder if we're on the news," said Kas. "Can we listen to the radio on your phone?"

"Not without a signal."

"We're stuffed, aren't we? Totally cut off."

"Of course not," said Jake. "As soon as we get within range of another tower, we'll start broadcasting our position again. It's not just Ouagadougou that has phone coverage, Kas. All the big towns do."

"What if they're not taking us to a big town? What if they're taking us to a tiny little village in the middle of nowhere? What if they're going to keep us as their slaves?"

What if? Jake wondered again who the Friends of the Poor

were, and why his father had sounded so strange on the phone. The group was an African branch of something bigger, he'd indicated. *A branch of what?*

"None of this would have happened if we had stayed away from the gold banquet," said Kas. "It's like this is our punishment for participating in the exploitation of African miners."

Right, that's it, thought Jake. "Like you care about African miners," he muttered.

"What?"

"You heard me. All you care about is having a nice big audience for the Daily Melodrama on Channel Kas."

"I can't believe you said that," whispered Kas. "I can't believe you think— Jake, what's happening? We're slowing down!"

The van braked hard and came to a stop. Jake shoved his phone into the back pocket of his trousers and listened, the hackles rising on his neck. *A door opening and closing. Footsteps coming around the side of the van, stopping by the back doors. The click of a key turning a lock. The creak of a hinge. A cruel, guttural voice.*

"*Descendez.* Get out."

Jake forced his bruised limbs to obey. Kirsty followed.

Countless stars filled the sky. In Ouagadougou the light pollution from houses and vehicles made it hard to see the stars, but out here in the bush they shone brightly. *Ad astra per aspera,* thought Jake. *Through adversity to the stars.*

The waiter stood before them. Jake kept his eyes lowered so as not to make eye contact. In the red glow of the van's taillights, the tattoo on the man's left forearm showed up clearly: a spider in its web, just as Kas had said.

"Let me introduce myself," said the man. "My name is Yakuuba Sor."

"What do you want?" asked Jake, keeping his eyes lowered.

"To start with," said Sor, "I want your phone."

"I don't have a phone."

Sor raised his fist and struck Jake hard across the face, making him stagger and fall. He heard a rush of white noise in his ears.

"I think you do," said Sor.

Ten

The grain merchants of Djibo had gathered in a private courtyard belonging to Al Hajji Amadou. They met every Tuesday at dead of night to fix their prices in time for Wednesday, which was the weekly market day. It had been seven months since last year's harvest, and the merchants knew that most people's granaries were now empty. This was the time of year when Al Hajji Amadou and his cronies were able to cash in on widespread hunger by pushing their grain prices sky-high.

They sat in a circle around a glowing kerosene lamp, talking loudly and laughing often. They passed a calabash of millet water around the circle, taking turns sipping the cool, floury liquid.

The Chameleon adjusted his disguise and rode through the archway into Al Hajji's courtyard. He tethered the sheikh's white stallion to a pillar, jumped down to the ground, and strode in among the grain merchants.

"So this is where hyenas go at night!" he cried, and his voice was that of a man ten years his elder.

Al Hajji Amadou jumped to his feet. "This is a private courtyard," he said. "Who are you?"

"My name," said the Chameleon, "is Sheikh Ahmed Abdullai Keita, Beloved of God, Friend of Djinns, Pillar of Righteousness! It is the djinns of the desert who have guided me into your foul midst."

"I have heard of you," murmured Al Hajji Amadou. "The prayer caller at the mosque tells me that you are a miracle worker." He approached the sheikh and offered him the calabash of millet water.

The Chameleon took a sip and passed the calabash back.

"The hour is late," said Al Hajji Amadou. "What do you want with us, holy man?"

The Chameleon shook his head from side to side so that his locks swung like pendulums. Then he began to laugh—a deep, resonant laugh. "The djinns of the desert mock you," he said. "Each week you meet here in the darkness, but the djinns see you as clear as day. You whisper your nefarious plans in each other's ears, unaware of the djinns who eavesdrop along the seams where earth meets heaven. You think you prosper, but tragedy is just a few short hours away."

Al Hajji Amadou frowned. "What tragedy?"

"You say to yourselves, *We are rich, we have everything we need, we will drive up the price of grain to cripple the poor. We will make them sell their animals to buy our grain. We will enrich ourselves at their expense. We will cruise on the river of their tears.*"

"What would the djinns have us do?"

"Halve and halve again the price of grain. Do not exceed a thousand francs a sack. This is the djinns' command."

The merchants chuckled at this preposterous idea. "The djinns have no head for business!" cried one, laughing so hard that he almost spilled the millet water in the calabash.

"Djinns don't need to eat," cried another. "If they did, they would know what a valuable commodity is a sack of millet!"

The Chameleon was the only man not laughing. "Woe to you who laugh now," he said. "Soon you will weep. Not one of you will sleep a wink tonight. You will sweat. You will toss and turn upon your beds. You will see the djinns with your own eyes. You will rise in the morning and go to market with all your limbs a-trembling, and if you do not price your millet according to the djinns' command, you will be cold in the ground by sunset."

Stunned silence followed. The merchants reeled from the force of these fighting words. Al Hajji Amadou glowered and pointed a quivering finger at the Chameleon. "Listen to me, miracle man. We buy our millet at a price and we sell it when and how we like. We are sophisticated, independent men, and we do not take orders from any saint or sprite."

"Brave words," said the Chameleon. "I wonder if they will be your last." He turned and ran back toward his stallion. "Behold!" he cried. "The djinns of the air are coming to bear me aloft on their warm, invisible hands." As he reached the place where the stallion was tethered, the Chameleon stopped and raised his arms.

The merchants held their breath. They did not notice the tiny clips that Paaté had sewn onto the Chameleon's "magic" moccasins. They did not notice the tiny shuffling movement with which he clipped the moccasins together. They did not notice him wriggling his left foot out of its shoe and poking his left leg forward through a discreet slit in his robes. They did not see him place the foot into the stallion's nearside stirrup. All they saw was a miracle that made them gasp and tremble. Seen from the back, the Chameleon's illusion was perfect: before their very eyes, the assembled grain merchants watched the famous sheikh rise into the air, hovering fully two feet off the ground.

The Chameleon floated up and forward and came to rest in the saddle of his horse. "Remember what I told you," he said.

"Not one of you will sleep a wink tonight. You will see the djinns with your own eyes. Be very careful how you price your millet at tomorrow's market. Do not exceed a thousand francs a sack." He flicked the reins, spurred his steed, and rode out into the street.

It had taken him a long time to work out how Sheikh Ahmed had performed his levitation in Mondoro, but in the middle of one sleepless night the answer had come to him: clips on the shoes, a slit in the robe, and something firm to step onto.

The Chameleon chuckled to himself. He was delighted to have given those shifty shopkeepers something to worry about. He was even more delighted to have a new illusion in his repertoire.

eleven

Sor allowed his hostages a two-minute toilet break and then ordered them back into the van. Jake felt sick at the thought of having to breathe that stale stock-cube air, but protesting would do no good. He helped his sister into the van and got in behind her. The doors slammed, and they were once more in darkness.

"I can't believe he hit you," said Kas. "That must have really hurt."

Jake touched his cheekbone and nodded.

"You should have handed it over straightaway. Dad said not to resist, remember?"

"It wasn't Dad's phone, it was mine! Besides, that phone was our best chance of rescue."

"Here's what I want to know," said Kas. "How did Sor know you had a phone?"

"Everyone has a phone."

"So why did he wait until now to take it from you?"

The question hung in the air, unanswerable.

Jake was expecting the van to start up again, but it did not. Soft footsteps trod close outside. Then there came a quiet hissing sound.

"Gas!" cried Kas. "They're going to gas us!"

Jake sniffed the air. At first all he could smell was the sickly chicken reek of artificial flavorings, but then he thought he detected a whiff of ethanol.

"It's not gas," he whispered. "It's paint. They're spray-painting the van."

They sat in the darkness and listened. Judging by the noises outside, the outlaws were doing more than just repainting the van. They were also changing the license plates and taking the amplifier off the roof. It was some time before the clattering of tools outside gave way to the quieter whirring of grasshoppers far out in the bush.

"How would you prefer to die?" asked Kas. "I mean, if you were given the choice."

"Kas, you're thirteen. You shouldn't be thinking about that sort of thing."

"All right, I'll narrow it down a bit."

"This isn't helping, Kas."

"Drowning or burning?"

"Kas!"

"Don't tell me you haven't thought about it."

"Fine. Drowning."

"Everyone says drowning." Kas sounded calmer now than she had all night, as if thinking about death were a comfort to her. "If I die and you survive, can you delete my Facebook account for me? My password is sultana5."

Jake lay down on the floor of the van and cradled his head in the crook of his arm. "No one's going to die, Kas."

"You say that, but you don't know. A girl at my school died of typhoid this term, and her Facebook page is still up. It's untidy."

Untidy. Jake shuddered. This was not the same Kas he had said goodbye to at Ouaga airport last Christmas. Was it Africa that had changed her, or was it this new obsession with all things emo?

He closed his eyes, and a succession of haunting images crowded into his mind. A walrus on a chair, a spider in its web, a pool attendant brandishing a leaf net, a delivery man silhouetted in the headlights of his van, Mungo Park escaping from the house of the wicked Moor and running, running, running, over the dunes . . .

"Crumbs!" shouted Kas.

Jake opened his eyes. He was lying on his side on the floor of the van, and his rib cage felt sore from the hard surface. The van was on the move again, but the ride was somehow smoother than before. *Sand*, thought Jake, and the words of the police commissioner came straight back to him. The desert is *beautiful, but dangerous.*

Something else was different, too. A ribbon of gray light was shining in under the back doors of the van. Daybreak.

Kas sat bolt upright. "Crumbs," she said again. "Breadcrumbs!" She crawled toward the back doors of the van and ran her finger along the ribbon of light at the base. "There's a gap," she said.

"Glad to hear it," said Jake, "because we don't know when our next toilet break is."

Kas grabbed one of the Jumbo stock cubes that had fallen onto the floor and unwrapped it. The wrapper was a small piece of yellow paper, adorned with the word JUMBO and a cartoon chicken.

"What are you going to do with that?" Jake asked.

"Advertise." Kas slotted the Jumbo wrapper into the gap under the door and helped it on its way with a flick of her nail. "I was just dreaming about Hansel and Gretel," she said. "Do you remember what they did? They laid a trail of breadcrumbs so that they could find their way back out of the forest."

"They didn't have GPS in those days," said Jake.

"And right now neither do we. Anyway, the trail's not for us, it's for anyone out there who's heard the news of our kidnapping. If they are announcing it on the radio, then people are going to be looking out for the Jumbo van, but they're not going to recognize it now that it's been repainted. Unless . . ."

"Unless it leaves a trail of Jumbo wrappers behind it," said Jake. "Nice one, Kas!"

"Steady on—we don't know if it'll work or not. But at least we'll feel like we're actually doing something. Do you want to unwrap or make the trail?"

"I'll unwrap."

There were thousands of stock cubes in the van. Jake unwrapped the tiny cubes as fast as he could and passed the wrappers to Kas, who flicked them through the narrow gap one at a time. They worked for more than an hour, and by the time they ran out of wrappers, their fingers were stiff and aching.

Jake sighed and leaned back against the mound of crumbly cubes. "Here's a question for you," he said. "If the van is traveling at thirty miles an hour, and you dropped an average of one Jumbo wrapper every five seconds, how far apart on the track are the wrappers?"

"Assuming that the wind speed remained constant," said Kas in a funny geeky voice, "I'd say, 'Just the right distance.'"

Jake chuckled. It was the first time he had laughed since they'd gotten kidnapped, and in that moment of forgetfulness he felt a spark of life returning to him.

Twelve

The sun rose over the corrugated roofs of Djibo, ancient seat of the Jelgooji kings. Outside a small shack on the outskirts of town, the Chameleon sat cross-legged on a straw mat with his cousin Badini. They were laughing so hard that tears ran down their faces.

"Behold," cried Badini. "The djinns are coming to bear me aloft!"

"On their warm, invisible hands!" chuckled the Chameleon.

"I would love to have seen Al Hajji Amadou's face when he saw you levitating."

"I'm telling you, cousin, he looked as if he'd swallowed an axe handle."

Badini guffawed and shook his head. "Seriously," he said. "Do you think it will work? Al Hajji Amadou and his friends are the most stiff-necked businessmen in town. They are sure to suspect a trick."

"The levitation was only half the story," said the Chameleon. "I also sprinkled deadly nightshade in their millet water."

"Deadly what?"

"It is a poison from beyond the Great Desert," said the Chameleon. "I purchased a small quantity from an Algerian merchant last market day. Don't look at me like that, cousin—the dose was not enough to kill them, only enough to make them pass a sleepless night of cold sweats and hallucinations."

"They will know you poisoned them."

"No, they won't. Nightshade powder does not make the lips or throat tingle as our local poisons do. Besides, cousin, you should never underestimate the power of suggestion. After my performance last night, every single merchant will think that desert djinns are tormenting him and will price his millet accordingly. The people of Djibo will be pleasantly surprised when they go to market today."

Badini got up, went into the house, and came back with a small radio. He set it down on the mat between him and his cousin. "Let us listen to the news," he said. "If all the grain merchants of Djibo have died mysteriously during the night, then you will have done a very bad thing and God will be your judge."

He switched on the radio and swiveled the antenna for best reception. On Radio Burkina a female presenter was speaking. "This crime has shocked the entire country. *Haut Commissaire* Beogo is here in the studio to tell us more. Commissioner, what progress are you making in your investigation?"

"*Bonjour*, Valérie. This is a heinous crime. It has prompted a nationwide investigation with unprecedented mobilization of police and *gendarmes*. We know that Yakuuba Sor is taking the hostages back to his camp somewhere in the north of the country, and we know that he is driving an orange and yellow Jumbo van. We are doing the best we can with very limited resources."

"How sure are you that Yakuuba Sor is behind this crime?"

"He was positively identified at the Jumbo depot yesterday morning when he stole the van and again at the Hotel Libya, the scene of the abduction. This would not be the first time that Sor has kidnapped high-ranking personages and held them hostage at his camp."

"He has never been known to kidnap a child, has he?"

"These are not children, Valérie. They are teenagers, and Sor would not think twice about targeting them. Our police psychologist tells us that Sor exhibits chronic psychotic tendencies. He is full of compassion one minute and utterly heartless the next. I cannot exaggerate the urgency of finding these unfortunate young people before it's too late."

"What has been the reaction of the British government?"

"Naturally, the British are extremely concerned, particularly by the link between Yakuuba Sor and a well-known international terrorist network. They have offered to assist our investigation in any way possible. We have applied to them for an injection of emergency antiterrorist funds and access to relevant surveillance technologies. Such equipment is vital if we are to effectively search that vast southern region of the Sahara Desert."

"Do you have a message for Yakuuba Sor?"

"We will find you, Sor. This time there is no ruse that can protect you, no disguise that can hide you, no desert hole that can conceal you. Make no mistake about it: shoulder to shoulder with our allies we will locate your camp, surround you, and crush you."

The Chameleon stood up, and his mouth was a thin, hard line. "Cousin Badini," he said, "I need you to go to the telecenter in Djibo and call our cells in Kongoussi, Namsigia, Woursé, Gaskindé, and Burizanga. Tell them to put the word out far and wide. If any man, woman, or child has seen that van, I want to know about it."

Thirteen

"**D**o you think anyone is going to notice our trail?" asked Kas for the third time in an hour.

"Definitely." Jake tried to sound more confident than he felt. "You know how observant African people are, especially in the bush. Anything even slightly out of the ordinary, they'll pick up on it. Tire tracks plus Jumbo wrappers plus radio broadcasts about the kidnapping. Pretty obvious, if you ask me. Hang on a second—are we slowing down again?"

The van stopped, the doors of the driver's cab clicked open, and slow footsteps came around the side of the van. Jake fingered the bruise on his cheek and wished that he were somewhere else.

The back doors of the van swung wide open. Jake and Kas blinked and winced, shielding their faces from the sudden brightness. One of their captors stood before them, silhouetted against the rising sun.

"*Salaam aleykum,*" he said.

"*Aleykum asalaam,*" replied Jake. *Don't make them angry,* he said to himself. *Don't whine. Don't be sarcastic. And whatever you do, don't look them in the eye.*

"*Descendez,*" said the man. It was Yakuuba Sor. He had wrapped a turban around his upper and lower face, leaving only a slit for his eyes. The waiter's bow tie hung loose around his neck, and on his left forearm the tattooed spider leered at Jake from its web.

Jake scrambled out of the van and dropped down onto the cool sand. He had never been in a desert before, and it was breathtaking. The lone undulating sands stretched far away in every direction. The sun hung low over the horizon and cast long, shifting shadows across the dunes.

Kas jumped down onto the sand behind him. Her hair, so black and sleek the night before, was a frizzy mess. Her face was pale, her eyes bloodshot. A trail of black eyeliner bisected each cheek. She was staring at something over Jake's shoulder.

Jake turned and saw the "delivery man," Sor's partner in

crime. He was still wearing his sunglasses, and in his arms he cradled a bolt-action hunting rifle with brass swirls on the stock. Jake turned away quickly. *So they do have a gun after all.*

Yakuuba Sor was peering into the back of the van, gazing at the mountains of crumbled-up stock cubes. *"C'est quoi, ça?"*

"We wanted something soft to sleep on," said Kas in French, her eyes fixed on the ground.

Sor scowled and walked up to her. "How old are you?" he asked.

"Thirteen." Her voice sounded tiny in that vast expanse.

"Can you read French?"

"Yes."

The outlaw took a sheet of paper from his pocket and handed it to her. "Go and stand over there," he said, waving at a spot a few meters away.

Kas went, walking stiff legged like a sleepwalker. She kept glancing out of the corner of her eye at the man with the rifle.

Sor held up the phone he had taken from Jake. "Does this take video?"

"Yes," said Jake.

"Good. You will film your sister while she reads."

Jake took the phone and noticed that it was now receiving a two-bar signal. *There must be a tower not very far away.*

"Start filming," said Sor.

Jake switched to video mode and framed his sister in the viewfinder. She was shaking like mad.

"Read," said the outlaw.

Kas began to read in a small, quavering voice. *"Je m'appelle Kirsty Knight—"*

"Louder!" shouted Sor. "Read it properly. And you, boy, are you filming?"

"Yes." Jake could feel the outlaw's breath on his neck.

Kas started again. "My name is Kirsty Knight, daughter of British ambassador Quentin Knight," she read in French. "My brother and I are guests of Yakuuba Sor and the Friends of the Poor. We are being treated kindly. Yakuuba Sor has only one demand, the release from British jails of the following men: Jamil al Rahabi, Ismail al Matari, Saad Salahuddin, Faruq Elgazzar, Tariq Dergoul, Ali al Nasir, and Sarfaraz Zaman. If the prisoners are released unharmed, my brother and I will also be released unharmed. There will be no negotiation. You have twenty-four hours to comply."

The video was forty-seven seconds long, and by the time he

pressed stop, Jake had lost all hope. He knew full well that the British government did not release prisoners in exchange for hostages. They were as good as dead.

Even Kas knew it. She started shaking again, and her breathing went funny. She looked like she was going to throw up.

"Play it back," said Sor.

Jake played the video, and the outlaws craned their necks to watch. The camera shake was terrible, but the speech was clearly audible.

"Post it online," said Sor.

"Whereabouts?"

"Facebook."

Jake logged onto his Facebook account and clicked new video. *Odd,* he thought, *that an outlaw in the Sahara Desert should know about social networking.*

There were loads of videos already on Jake's profile. There were clips of him geothimbling, skateboarding, pillow fighting, moshing, arm wrestling, conjuring, and (for some reason he had long forgotten) singing "Poker Face" through a mouthful of marshmallows. And in about three minutes' time, connection permitting, there would be a new one—a video of Kas on a bad hair day, reading out the demands of a madman. *If the prisoners are released unharmed, my brother and I will also be released un-harmed. There will be no negotiation. You have twenty-four hours to comply.*

"Is it done yet?" said Sor. "Have you done what I asked?" He kept looking up at the horizon, and the brow line of his tur-ban was damp with perspiration.

"It's a large file," said Jake. "It will take a little while."

The delivery man seemed nervous too. He gripped the rifle tight and shifted his weight from foot to foot.

"Is it done yet?" snapped Sor again. "Can we go?"

"Not yet." The blue progress bar was edging forward, but the battery level was critical. The phone was about to die on them.

"*Allons-y!*" said the delivery man. "We have to leave right now."

"Not yet," said Sor. "Tell me, boy, is the upload finished?"

"It's finished."

"Good." Sor snatched the phone and pocketed it. "Go and stand next to your sister."

Jake went.

"Kneel down, both of you," said Sor.

"What?"

"Just do it."

"You said in the video that we had twenty-four hours!"

"Kneel down!" screamed the outlaw.

Jake and Kas knelt.

Sor turned to his accomplice. "Kill them," he said.

FOURTEEN

The delivery man took a clip of five rifle cartridges from his shirt pocket. He drew the bolt back to open the breech, top-loaded the clip, and pushed the bolt forward and down.

"If you kill us," stuttered Jake, "our government will send soldiers and planes. They will not rest until the Friends of the Poor are completely destroyed."

The delivery man raised the rifle to his shoulder.

"Please, no," said Kas. "Don't shoot." Her panda eyes were wide open, staring at the barrel of the rifle. She was hyperventilating, her nostrils flaring and collapsing with alarming speed. "I should have eaten the gold," she sobbed. "I should have eaten the gold."

Jake put an arm around his sister and closed his eyes tight. "Don't be daft," he whispered. "Everyone knows that eating gold is bad for you."

Please God, he thought, *don't let this hurt.* A bluish glow meandered across the retinas of his closed eyes where the rising sun had made its impression. *Mungo Park died young too. Also from a gunshot wound. Came under fire at the Bussa Rapids. Nothing he could do. Died on the river he mapped.*

Death was taking its time. Jake opened his eyes a fraction.

Sor's accomplice was still standing over them, but he had lowered the rifle slightly and was staring into the distance. Jake turned and saw a wisp of dust rising in the air behind a faraway dune. The sound of drumming reached his ears.

"Qu'est-ce que c'est?" murmured the delivery man.

"Never mind that," said Sor. "Kill the children, quickly."

The man with the rifle hesitated, his eyes still fixed on the horizon. "Hooves," he said.

He was not wrong. Up over the dune came a posse of horsemen, galloping hard with the sun on their backs and spraying sand on either side. The delivery man gripped his rifle and glanced at Sor for reassurance.

"Do it!" shouted Sor.

"I can't. We were told no witnesses."

Told by who? thought Jake. *Who are they taking their orders from?*

There were five horses, matching one another stride for stride. They were about half a mile away and closing fast, their hooves like thunder on the morning air.

"Give me the rifle!" cried Sor. "You go and start the engine. Driving is all you're good for."

The delivery man handed over his weapon and hurried back to the van. Sor lifted an arm to wipe the perspiration from his eyes and raised the rifle to his right shoulder.

"Five witnesses," murmured Jake in French.

Sor scowled. "What did you say?"

"Nothing. It just seems like a lot of witnesses, that's all."

The outlaw stepped forward and cracked Jake around the head with the stock of the rifle. Then he raised the rifle to his shoulder, lined up the sight posts, and fired. Sand puffed up in front of the oncoming horsemen; the bullet had fallen short. He cycled the bolt and fired again—closer this time, but the horses charged on relentless without even breaking their stride.

Yakuuba Sor looked at the ambassador's children and back at the galloping horses. "I'll deal with you two later," he said. "Get in the van, both of you."

Jake and Kas scuttled to the van and jumped into the back. The vehicle revved loudly, its wheels spinning in the sand. Instead of slamming the doors behind his hostages, Sor climbed in behind them. He closed one door and propped the other one wide open with his foot.

"Give me space," said Sor. "Back against the partition, both of you."

The van lurched forward, accelerating fast across the white sand. Jake and his sister shuffled backward into the shadows, and as they did so, Jake noticed with surprise that the edges of Sor's spiderweb tattoo were smudged. *That's no tattoo,* he thought. *That's ink.*

A deafening bang echoed inside the van, and a wisp of smoke rose from the barrel of Sor's rifle. Kas screamed and hugged her knees. Jake edged to one side until he could see the horses. On they came, undeterred by the gunshot, splitting the wind with their furious pace—two chestnuts, two blacks, and a copper-colored one. They were no more than a quarter of a mile away.

The outlaw fired again, and once again a puff of sand flew up right in front of the horses' feet. The riders responded by breaking their tight formation and fanning out across the wide expanse of sand.

"I can't look," said Kirsty. She had her fingers in her ears and her eyes tight shut.

"Fine," said Jake. "Just keep your head down." *Who are these horsemen?* he wondered. *They don't look like state police. Why should they risk their necks on behalf of foreigners?*

One of the riders seemed to stretch out his hands toward the van. Something sang through the air and right into the van, pinging against the partition next to Jake's left arm. A stone. These five madmen were riding against a loaded rifle armed with nothing more dangerous than *slingshots*.

Yakuuba Sor shoved another cartridge clip into the magazine, braced himself against the side of the van, and raised the rifle to his shoulder. Another small stone whizzed past, grazing his right ear. He bellowed in fury and fired off all five rounds one after another, the empty cartridges plinking onto the floor of the van.

The van drove up onto an expanse of flat rock and accelerated hard through the gears. The horses shortened their stride and began to fall behind, their hooves clattering weakly on the hard surface.

"What's going on?" said Kas.

"The horses don't like the rock," said Jake. "I think we're losing them."

When the rocky plateau came to an end, the van careered back down onto sand, and this time it was a soft, fine sand that sucked at the tires and made the engine scream. The van plowed the sand in low gear and plunged onward up a steep incline.

"Dunes!" Jake shouted. "Hang on tight, Kas!"

Around one, over the next. On every incline, a jumble of loose crates and stock cubes went slithering out of the open door of the van. On every dune crest the vehicle seemed to grow wings, airborne for a few heady, stomach-churning moments before landing with a slam and a metallic groan.

Jake heard the distant thud of hooves on sand, and suddenly there they were again, two blacks and two chestnuts, gaining fast about two dunes back, falling out of view and then rising again, surfing the desert waves with speed and poise.

The riders gripped their mounts with their knees and, as they got close, began once more to fire their slingshots. One stone after another fizzed through the air. Most were falling short, but a couple hit the door of the Nissan or ricocheted off the tailgate. Slowly but surely the shooters were finding their range again.

The outlaw loaded another clip into his rifle and returned fire as best he could, but only an expert marksman could have coped with this jolting thirty-mile-an-hour shootout.

"There were five horses a minute ago," said Kas. "What happened to the bay?"

"The what?"

"The bay—the copper-colored horse with the black mane and tail. There were five horses and now there are only four."

They soon had their answer. As the van hurled itself around the side of the next dune, the missing bay swung suddenly into view from behind the open door, racing at full gallop. Jake saw flared nostrils, the glint of a bit, and the taut rubber of a slingshot.

Sor did not even have time to gasp. A small, smooth stone hit him just above his right eye, and he slumped unconscious on the floor of the van.

The rider was only a boy—he looked about Jake's age. He was sitting high on the horse's neck like a race jockey. *"Waru ga!"* shouted the boy, gesturing wildly.

Jake crawled over to Sor and retrieved his phone from the outlaw's pocket.

"I think he's telling us to jump," said Kas. "He must be crazy."

"Waru ga!" repeated the boy rider.

"It'll be fine," said Jake. "Just keep your arms tight to your body and jump in the direction of travel."

"And you've jumped from a moving vehicle before, have you?"

87

Jake never had, but he had read a thing or two about how it was done. Earlier in the year, he had downloaded an SAS extreme survival manual onto his phone and read it during double algebra. So what he lacked in the quadratic equations department he made up for in survival know-how. He knew that if you are being chased by a crocodile, you should run in zigzags, and if you are performing an emergency tracheotomy, you should use a clean ballpoint pen, and if you have to jump from a moving vehicle, you should keep your arms tight to your body and roll—unless you want your limbs to snap like twigs.

"I'll go first," said Jake. "Just watch me and do what I do."

"Wait!" cried Kas. "We don't know anything about these boys. They could be even worse than Sor for all we know."

But Jake had already made up his mind. He stepped out onto the tailgate of the van, shut his eyes tight, tucked in his arms, and leaped.

FIFTEEN

Jake felt a rush of warm air and then hit the sand at thirty miles an hour. The SAS extreme survival manual had mentioned nothing about how much the rolling would hurt. It was like turning somersaults on an industrial sander.

When he finally came to a stop and opened his eyes, the bay was standing over him, lustrous flanks heaving from the strenuous gallop. Her nostrils were flared, her eyes bright, her ears pricked. Mounted on her back was the African boy who had downed Yakuuba Sor. He had short straight hair and a long scar along one cheek. A slingshot dangled from his hand.

"*Salaam aleykum*," said the boy.

Jake did not reply. He got to his feet and half ran, half hobbled to where his sister lay curled up on the sand. "Kas!" he cried. Her banquet dress was ripped and her bare elbows were bleeding. "Kas! Kas!"

"That's my name," she mumbled. "Don't wear it out."

Jake looked up. The delivery man must have seen them jump. He had turned the van around and was heading their way fast.

"Come on!" shouted Jake. "We need to get out of here."

The five horsemen—horseboys, rather, for not one of them looked older than sixteen—formed a protective circle around Jake and his sister, slingshots at the ready. As soon as the van came within range, they began to fire. A barrage of stones hit the windshield, cracking it in several places.

Two of the lads shuffled backward on their horses to make room for the extra riders. Jake helped his sister onto the back of one of the chestnuts. Then he leaped sideways onto the bay and braced himself for the off. The boys let loose a final volley of stones from their slingshots.

The van's windshield fractured into a mosaic of tiny shards, but the driver did not slow down. Instead he used his elbow to punch a hole in the shattered glass. The boys flicked their reins, and the horses shot off at a heart-stopping pace, jostling for position in their eagerness to flee from the oncoming vehicle. Fire in their bellies, they flared their nostrils, strained at their bits, and galloped into the heart of the wind.

Jake was as terrified as the horses, maybe more. His only

experience of riding had been donkeys in Scarborough, but the crazed animal on which he now sat was more suited to a rodeo than a beach.

As the bay lunged forward, fast and wild, Jake was possessed of a quaking fear and a strong urge to jump off. *Calm down*, he told himself. *Calm down and concentrate.* As they picked up speed, he leaned back a little and lifted his left leg across the shimmering mane to straddle the bay properly. It felt more secure this way but also more uncomfortable. The bay was lean, and sitting astride her bony back was like perching on a banister. The saddle, a scratchy blanket folded double, did little to cushion the ride.

Behind Jake, the boy urged on his steed with loud guttural cries, handling the reins with a confidence that suggested many years of bareback riding. The other horses fanned out behind him, riding in a wide V formation. But the sandy terrain was giving way to rock, and here the horses were no match for the Nissan. It was already on the tail of the hindmost horse.

The frantic animal bucked and swerved to one side, an instant too late. The van's bumper clipped a trailing hoof and sent horse and rider sprawling onto the rocks. The rider only just managed to roll clear of the Nissan's tires.

The four remaining riders used their slingshots as whips to spur their horses on, and Jake clung tight to the horse's mane. The rock before them stretched to a distant horizon. Glancing over his shoulder, Jake saw the van close on the heels of the second chestnut—*Kas's horse!* The driver's lips were parted in a sadistic grin. He was going to show no mercy.

"*Gooruwol!*" cried the boy in front, gathering up the reins and pushing Jake forward onto the horse's neck. The animal jumped, and only when she was airborne did Jake see the reason why. They had come to a wadi—a dry riverbed, cutting unexpectedly across their path. One by one, the horses leaped, bunching up their muscles and powering off their back legs to clear the sandy chasm.

The Nissan could not leap. By the time the driver braked, it was already far too late. The van careered straight down into the wadi and crashed headfirst into the far bank. Its hood crumpled like an aluminum can, and the driver flew face first through the windshield. Steam hissed angrily from the radiator. Blood spattered the sand.

Jake took one look at the mangled body and his stomach lurched. The delivery man would not be making any deliveries next week. Maybe not ever. Of the van's other occupant, Yakuuba Sor, there was no sign.

With the chase over, the horses settled from their frenzied gallop into an insistent driving canter. Straining her head forward, the bay attacked the ground before her with magnificent long strides, her flanks slick with sweat, hot wind whistling in her nostrils. When they had put sufficient distance between themselves and the crash, they slowed to a gentle single-file walk. The horse that had fallen rejoined the group. Horse and rider were unhurt.

Kas was two horses behind Jake, pale and shaking.

"*Salaam aleykum,*" said the boy who had rescued him.

"*Bonjour,*" said Jake. "Do you speak French?"

"*Munya tan faa kooten tafon,*" said the boy. The language was not Arabic and it was certainly not French.

"What is your name?" asked Jake.

"*Mi faamaay,*" said the boy. It did not sound like a name. It was more likely to mean "I don't understand" or "shut up." Then again, he had to call the boy something.

"Farm Eye," said Jake. "Thank you for rescuing us."

Farm Eye took from his top pocket a wad of Jumbo chicken-stock-cube wrappers and waved them in front of Jake's nose.

Nice one, Kas, thought Jake. *Your Hansel and Gretel breadcrumb trail worked.* But his relief at being rescued was tinged with deep uncertainty. Was this really a rescue? As Kas had pointed out, they did not know a single thing about this cowboy posse. For all they knew, the boys might be even worse than Sor and his lot. Jake had heard horrifying stories about Africa's brutal teenage gangs: the Bakassi Boys of Igbo, the Area Boys of Lagos, the West Side Junglers of Sierra Leone. A wave of fear and nausea passed over him. They had avoided being killed by Yakuuba Sor, it was true, but there were worse things than death.

"I'm thirsty," he said, cupping his hand in front of his mouth in what he imagined to be the international sign language for water.

"*Ndiyam walaa,*" muttered Farm Eye, shaking his head.

"Jake!" called Kas. "What's going on? Are they taking us back to Ouagadougou?"

"No. Sun's behind us and on the right, which means we're still going north."

"Have you got a signal on your phone?"

"The battery's dead."

The five horses climbed a dune in single file and began to trot along the crest. Far away on the eastern horizon was what Jake had been looking for: a jumble of mud-brick rooftops, a cluster of trees, the minaret of a mosque, the shimmer of a lake, and a cell phone tower.

"A town!" shouted Kas. "Do you think it's got a police station?"

Jake turned to Farm Eye and pointed east. *"Allons-y,"* he said. "Let's go there."

The boy nodded. "Kongoussi," he said, but he showed no sign of straying from his northerly course.

"We want to go to the police station in Kongoussi," repeated Jake. "Can you take us there, please?"

Farm Eye shook his head. *"Geddal wi'ii dey, sannaa min njaara on tomakko."*

Jake suddenly shifted in the saddle and brought his left leg up as if to dismount, but Farm Eye was having none of it. In one quick movement he gathered up the slack in the reins, looped it twice around Jake's wrists, and pulled tight. Then he jabbed his heel against the bay's side, spurring her into a trot.

Jake stared at his bound wrists. The looped reins formed simple, painless handcuffs, but handcuffs all the same. If he tried to dismount now, he would end up getting dragged along, or worse.

They trotted down the side of the dune and onto the flat. Farm Eye gave the bay her head, and she broke once more into a swift rolling canter. Canter, trot, walk, canter, trot, walk—

that was the cycle, repeated over and over during the course of the next three hours. The sun was high and blisteringly hot. Jake's mouth was parched, his lips were cracked, and his head ached. Once or twice he saw a herder in the distance, but his mouth was so dry that his attempted cries for help came out as little more than croaks.

Jake wanted to be brave for his sister's sake, but he was feeling a growing sense of desperation. They were still being held against their will. They had no idea who their new captors were, or what they might want, or where they were going. All they could be sure of were the twin torments of dehydration and sunburn. His ears, nose, and neck would be agony in the morning.

"*Accana kam hakke,*" said Farm Eye.

Jake turned in the saddle just in time to see his captor bring a long piece of blue cloth down over his head. It was an indigo turban, like the ones worn by camel herders. Farm Eye wound the turban around and around Jake's head, over his ears, nose, mouth, forehead, and chin.

At first he was grateful for the covering. Perhaps Farm Eye had noticed his sunburned skin and wanted to protect him. Only when Farm Eye began to wrap the turban around Jake's eyes did Jake realize that this was more than a sun hat. It was a blindfold.

"Kas," called Jake, and his tongue felt thick and swollen in his mouth. "What's going on?"

But the voice that came out of his mouth was inaudible to anyone but himself—a dust-dry whisper muffled in folds of indigo.

Sixteen

At the British embassy in Ouagadougou, a meeting was taking place between Ambassador Quentin Knight and MI6 officer Roy Dexter. The spy had arrived at nine o'clock that morning on an emergency overnight flight from London. Dexter's eyes were blue, his jaw was square, and his long, sunbleached hair was tied back in a ponytail.

"Thank you for coming," said Mr. Knight, shaking hands. "I trust that you have been fully briefed by the Foreign Office."

"Two missions," said Dexter briskly. "Rescue the children and disincentivize Yakuuba Sor."

"Disincentivize?"

"Kill."

The ambassador pursed his lips. He himself would have

chosen a different word—terminate, perhaps—but now was no time to split hairs. "Be careful, Dexter," he said. "Yakuuba Sor is a slippery customer, by all accounts. He is a master of disguise and a ruthless killer."

"I know," said Dexter.

As a long-serving diplomat, Mr. Knight was highly experienced in the reading of body language and microexpressions. He could not help noticing the momentary emotion that flashed across the officer's face.

The ambassador came right out with it. "Are you frightened, Dexter?"

"What?"

"I mean to say, it would be perfectly natural if you were."

A muscle twitched in the man's jaw. "I have a healthy respect for terrorists, yes. I have had some unpleasant encounters in the past, one in particular. Turkmenistan. I was captured."

"I see."

"It was completely my own fault," continued Dexter. "I was naive. I gave a man the benefit of the doubt when I should have given him a bullet in the head. I will not repeat that mistake."

"Of course not."

Dexter turned away and fumbled with the latches on his

briefcase. He opened it and removed a small round tin of hard candies. "As you know," he said, "the Burkina Faso police have requested help with counterterrorist surveillance. Since you have already signed the Official Secrets Act, I can trust you to tell no one about the contents of this tin." He lifted the lid.

Mr. Knight stood up and leaned across his desk to look. In the tin, gnawing on a leaf, was an insect. It was about four centimeters long, and its exoskeleton was reddish brown.

"HI-MEMS," said Dexter. "Hybrid Insect-Micro-Electro-Mechanical System."

"Looks to me like a beetle."

"A rhinoceros beetle, to be precise," said the spy. "But this particular rhinoceros beetle is worth about eight grand. She has a one-megapixel camera on her head, twenty-eight solar cells on her thorax, and a miniature GPS on her abdomen. Sexy, huh?"

"Profoundly."

"Ever since the start of the Iraq war, the boffins at HQ have been attempting to make a surveillance droid that is tiny, controllable, and capable of relaying images from the harshest environments in the world. They tried all sorts of miniature flying vehicles, but nothing they could make was as stable or as powerful as a real live insect. So guess what they did! They started using real, live insects! They implanted microchips into beetle larvae in the early stages of metamorphosis, intertwining the nerves and muscles with electronic circuitry. In effect, they were creating the world's first bioelectrical surveillance droids."

"Cyborgs."

"Correct, Mr. Knight. And this particular cyborg is going to find your kids."

The ambassador watched the rhinoceros beetle shuffling in its leafy prison. He had heard of the HI-MEMS project some years ago but had not believed it would come to anything. "Capital," he murmured. "And how will the cyborg know where Jake and Kirsty are?"

"That's easy. As soon as Jake's phone starts getting reception again, we can use the tower ID to locate him to within a mile or two. I then get myself to the edge of that zone and release Xena."

"Who?"

"The beetle. Xena has two neural stimulators implanted in her brain and two in her wings, to direct her flight. As she flies, she will relay signals to and from your son's phone, pinpointing his position with ever-increasing accuracy. At the same time, she will be relaying her video back to me. Positioning and surveillance in one pretty little package. Do you want to know the best bit?"

"Hit me."

"Xena is completely invisible."

"I beg your pardon?"

"Think about it, Mr. Knight. In every square mile of West Africa there are more than five billion insects. Xena could fly right past Yakuuba Sor's nose and he wouldn't see a thing."

seventeen

Slumped forward on the neck of the bay, Jake had no idea how long they had been traveling. His groin ached. His ribs ached. Most of all, his head ached. Only last night he had been ranting about how much he wanted to visit the deserts of the north. Now that he was here, he longed to be anywhere else. Commissioner Beogo's words about the desert throbbed in his memory: *It is beautiful, but dangerous. My people say that the deserts of the north are a battlefield for angels and demons.*

Bound up inside his turban, he began to hallucinate. He saw ranks of translucent angels and shaggy-haired demons lining up against each other on a rocky plateau. The demons held heavy wooden quarterstaffs, which they thudded on the rock in rhythmic fury. The angels swayed in unison and clapped their slender hands.

THUD-THUD, clap-clap, THUD-THUD, clap-clap.

Farm Eye unwound Jake's turban and uncovered his eyes. The harsh glare of the sun skewered his retinas, and he cried out in pain. But what he saw when his eyes adjusted to the light sickened him even more—an acacia tree with a bloodied carcass hanging from its branches. The glazed eyes and drooping ears seemed to be those of a goat. Two teenage boys armed with machetes were busy skinning the body, and blood was dripping onto the sand beneath. Farther away Jake saw more carcasses lying on the ground, indistinct beneath clouds of flies. He dry retched and looked around for his sister. There she was, two horses back, still slumped over the neck of the chestnut stallion. She seemed to be asleep.

Lucky her. This was no time to be awake.

They had entered a large dust bowl surrounded by high dunes. On the right a camel with a harness around its neck was being made to draw water from a deep well. On the left was a cluster of domed huts that seemed to be made out of straw matting. On the sandy path ahead scrawny chickens fled the oncoming hooves, and still that eerie thudding sounded in Jake's ears.

THUD-THUD, clap-clap, THUD-THUD, clap-clap.

The horses walked on unperturbed. They passed by two enclosures, bounded by fences woven out of thorny branches. The first enclosure was full of goats. In the second three horses and their teenage riders were being put through their paces on an improvised target range. The boys were riding in wide circles, and as they reached the east end of the enclosure, they fired off slingshots at a selection of eight objects balanced on wooden stakes: three tin cans, two plastic bottles, a baobab fruit, a conical hat, and a rusty metal teapot. Each boy fired eight stones as he cantered past the targets, and there were far more hits than misses.

The bay got excited when she saw the cantering horses. She bucked and pranced and threw her head from side to side. Farm Eye reined her in with a firm hand, digging in his spurs to move her on.

They came now to the center of the settlement, where there stood a huge white canvas marquee with a red cross on each wall. *Free gift from the people of Norway* read the slogan above the doorway. Jake wondered how the people of Norway would feel to know that their gift to the Red Cross had ended up as the centerpiece of a terrorist training camp.

In the afternoon shade on the east side of the marquee stood three large wooden mortars, the source of all that thudding. Six teenage boys, each wielding a thick wooden pestle as tall as himself, were pounding the contents of the mortars with ferocious energy. Each boy threw his pounding stick into the air between downstrokes and clapped his hands before catching it again. Jake had seen women pounding grain on his previous visits to Burkina Faso, but he had never seen it done by a man or a boy.

As the hostage convoy passed by, the pounding sticks froze in mid-swing like the worn-out pistons of some giant engine. The boys' frank, appraising stares made Jake uneasy, and he thought again about the goat carcass hanging from the tree. His bound hands trembled in his lap.

The horses passed a line of shade shelters and two mud-brick huts before arriving at an enormous baobab tree whose bulbous stubby branches cast sinister shadows on the sand. Farm Eye clicked his tongue and brought the bay to a halt. He unbound Jake's wrists and helped him to dismount.

Jake's knees were so weak with fear and tension that he could hardly stand. He had to support himself with one hand on the horse's back. As for Kas, she was still asleep, slumped forward over the chestnut stallion's neck.

From all over the settlement, teenage boys approached. They came from the Red Cross tent, from the training ring, from shade shelters and grass huts. Jake looked around at the rows of upturned faces and bit his lip hard in an effort to suppress his fear. *Bakassi Boys, Area Boys, West Side Junglers. There are worse things than death.*

Jake had visited African villages before, and what usually struck him were the hordes of small children shouting *Ça va? Ça va?* or demanding a *cadeau* in the form of a Bic or a balloon or a Matchbox car. This village was different. There was not a single child here under the age of ten.

Terrorists, thought Jake. *Outlaw terrorists. Outlaw terrorist cannibals with slingshots.*

The occupants of the settlement were mostly boys, but not entirely. An African girl sashayed through the crowd holding two calabashes full of water. She wore a white cotton dress, her long hair was arranged in intricate jeweled braids, and around her neck hung a silver pendant and a slingshot. She stopped in front of Jake and offered him a drink.

Water. Jake's hands were shaking so much that he could hardly hold the calabash. He raised the bowl to his dry, cracked lips and gulped the murky brown liquid. Buckets of water arrived for the horses, too. Farm Eye's mare lowered her majestic head and slurped, her slick flanks heaving from the exertion of the journey.

Already Jake could feel that the water was doing him good.

He felt it permeating his whole body, from cell to thirsty cell, refreshing and reviving as it went. His skin tingled as a myriad of pores opened and perspired at long, long last. He gasped, wiped his sleeve across his mouth, and handed back an empty bowl.

"Tuubaaku walaa semteende," muttered Farm Eye, and he shot the white boy a contemptuous glance.

The girl in the white dress took the bowl and looked at Jake with narrowed eyes and a Mona Lisa smile. *"Bonjour,"* she said. To Jake's relief she spoke in French. "My name is Mariama."

"Bonjour," said Jake. "Where are we?"

"We are in the desert," said the girl. "The precise location is a secret, which is why you were blindfolded."

"Why so secret?"

"Outlaws have many enemies." She went over to Kas, who was still sleeping, and touched her lightly on the cheek.

"Don't hurt her," said Jake.

Mariama leaned close to the sleeping girl and whispered in her ear.

Kas stirred, blinked, and looked around. Immediately there was panic in her eyes. "Jake, tell me where we are," she blurted out. "Who are all these people? Why are they staring at me?"

"They're outlaws," said Jake in English.

"No," said Kas. "No, no." As if saying no could make it not true.

"Take this," said Jake, handing her a calabash passed to him by one of the boys. "You need to drink."

"I want to go home," mumbled Kas. She looked groggy and confused.

"Enough," said Mariama. "Be quiet and follow me."

"Where to?"

"To the Needle Hut."

The Needle Hut was a mud-brick building west of the baobab tree. It housed three antique-looking sewing machines and a wooden workbench laden with needles, thread, sequins, zippers, scissors, clothes hangers, assorted rolls of brightly colored cotton cloth, and a shortwave radio. The floor was carpeted with offcuts of fabric, and swaths of sand blew in through the open doorway. Seated at one of the sewing machines was a weasely boy wearing a purple robe and a baseball cap. He looked about eighteen.

"Stop what you are doing, Paaté," said Mariama in French. "Our red-eared guests want robes."

The tailor looked at Kirsty's and Jake's torn, dust-caked clothes and tutted loudly. He switched on the radio, picked up a tape measure from the workbench, and beckoned to Jake. As he measured, the radio news came on in French:

"The investigation continues into last night's kidnapping of two British children. The children, whose father is British ambassador Quentin Knight, were abducted in a Jumbo van driven by the notorious Saharan outlaw Yakuuba Sor. The British embassy received from Sor a hostage video demanding the immediate release of seven convicted terrorists currently held in British jails. In response, Ambassador Knight has been holding a press conference. He offered a reward of two hundred thousand African francs for information leading to the safe return of his children. In other news . . ."

Paaté showed no interest in the news report. When he had finished taking Jake's and Kirsty's measurements, he led them back out into the blazing sunlight. They went past the baobab tree, the Red Cross tent, and the goat enclosure, and finally arrived at a tiny domed hut made of grass matting.

The tailor pointed at the low doorway. "In you go," he said. "Eat some *nyiiri,* drink some milk, wash yourselves, and sleep. There is washing water and soap in the bucket behind the hut. Any questions?"

"Yes," said Jake. "Who is in charge here?"

"The Chameleon," said Paaté. "He has gone to Djibo market. He will be back this evening."

"Which way is Djibo?" said Jake.

Paaté scowled and waggled his finger in front of Jake's nose. "If you try to escape," he said, "you will die in the desert. Wait here for the Chameleon. He will be back tonight."

eighteen

Jake had to get down on his hands and knees to enter the grass hut, and even when he got inside, it was too low for him to stand. He looked around. The framework of the hut was simplicity itself: fifteen long, thin branches planted in a circle and curving inward to a central apex. The walls and ceiling were made of straw, loosely woven to let in the breeze. Most of the space inside the hut was taken up by a bed—a towering stack of wide grass mats.

Kas followed Jake in and sat on the edge of the bed.

"He's right," whispered Jake. "If we try to escape, we will die in the desert."

"Whatever," said Kas. She was sitting on her hands, staring straight ahead of her.

"Crazy day, huh?" whispered Jake. "That sun was a nightmare."

"Yes."

"Did you hear the radio just now? Dad's offered a reward for any information that leads to our rescue."

"Yup."

"On a scale of one to ten, how sore is your butt right now?"

Kas put her face in her hands and began to cry softly. "Nine and a half," she said.

Jake put an arm around her. He did not say anything for fear of crying himself.

"You always wanted to have a real adventure," sobbed Kas. "How are you liking it?"

"Not much," said Jake. "I always reckoned that if ever a real adventure came along, I'd be a bit—you know . . ."

"A bit what?"

Jake shrugged and looked away. "A bit braver."

"A bit more like Mungo what's-his-name?"

"Yes."

Hanging above the bed was a shallow wicker basket containing a metal plate, a wooden spoon, a box of matches, and a flashlight. On the white sand at the foot of the bed were two wooden bowls. One was full of milk; the other contained a crusty gray paste. This, presumably, was the *nyiiri* that Paaté had recommended.

"I suppose we should eat something," Jake said. They had eaten nothing but stock cubes since the banquet. He picked up a handful of *nyiiri* and bit some off. It was cold and chewy but not unpleasant.

Kas picked up the calabash of goat's milk. "We almost got killed today," she said, talking between sips. "Those men were totally going to shoot us."

"I still don't get it," said Jake. "If Sor's the leader of his gang, who told him to make sure there were no witnesses? And another thing," he continued, waving a handful of *nyiiri* in the air. "Why is his tattoo not a tattoo?"

"I don't know." Kas shrugged and lay back on the bed. "My brain hurts."

"Back in a minute," said Jake. "I'm going for a wash." He crammed one last glob of *nyiiri* into his mouth and crawled through the low doorway into the fierce sunlight. Around the back of the hut there was a bucket of water and soap, just as Paaté had said. Jake crouched naked on the hot sand and used a plastic mug to pour water over himself. The water felt cool on his sunburned skin.

By the time Jake got dry and dressed, Kas was fast asleep. He lay down beside her and stared up at the wicker basket hanging above his head. Out of habit more than anything else, he took the phone from his pocket and tried switching it on. Nothing. Not even a flicker.

He glanced down at the calabash of goat's milk and an idea came to him—not so much an idea as a memory, a clip he had seen on YouTube a few weeks before. He jumped off the bed and grabbed the metal plate and the flashlight from the hanging basket. He flicked the flashlight on, just to check that it was working, and then, with shaking fingers, he opened the battery compartment. He slid the batteries out, placed them side by side in the center of the metal plate, and turned his attention to the milk. It would need to be thicker, that milk.

There was an old gourd by the entrance to the hut—it was about the size of a soccer ball, and its hard exterior had been worn smooth by years of use. Gourds and calabashes came from the same plant family, Africa's answer to Tupperware. Jake poured the goat's milk into the gourd, covered the open neck with his hand, and began to shake. At first the milk sloshed thinly, but after a few minutes of churning, it began to feel different. Soon it was slap-slapping against the sides of the gourd so loudly that it woke Kas.

"What are you doing?" asked Kas.

"I'm trying to charge my phone," said Jake. "Don't make that face—I'm being serious. Not a lot of people know this, but milk is a great conductor of electricity."

Jake tipped over the gourd and strained the contents through his fingers so that he was left with a handful of thick butter. Then he smothered the butter all over the batteries until they were completely sealed in. He took the USB cable from his money belt, dipped one end into the butter, and attached the other end to his phone. For a moment nothing happened. Then the screen of the phone lit up, and a "battery charging" icon appeared.

Kas squealed and punched the air. "You're a genius!"

"Don't thank me," said Jake. "Thank YouTube."

"I can't believe it worked."

"Simple physics," said Jake, sliding the whole contraption out of sight behind the bed. "Should take about three hours to fully charge."

Jake slept fitfully. He dreamed of harsh desert landscapes, shaggy-haired demons, and killer bees. The demons kept prodding him with their quarterstaffs, and the bees prodded him with their evil barbed stings. He could not get comfortable whichever way he lay.

"There's still no signal on your phone."

"What?" Jake opened his eyes and frowned up at the straw dome above his head. For a moment he had no idea where he was, but he soon remembered all too well. His legs and lower back were aching from the morning's ride, and his sunburned nose and cheeks stung like mad.

Kas was sitting on the edge of the bed, washed and dressed in a loose cotton robe. She was still wearing her skull-bow necklace from the gold banquet. The enamel pendant hanging from the necklace depicted a grinning white skull topped with a jaunty bow. "Your phone charged all right," she said, "but there's no signal."

"Did you try it outside?"

"Course."

"What time is it?"

"Evening."

Jake yawned and sat up. "What on earth is that?" he said, looking at Kas's robe.

"There's clothes for you, too," said Kas. "Mariama brought them while you were sleeping. She brought us flip-flops, too. She said there's going to be a banquet in the Red Cross tent tonight."

Jake got changed quickly. The new trousers were a good fit, but the robe came all the way down to his knees. "I feel like Wee Willie Winkie," he complained.

"Get used to it," said Kas. "Come on, let's go."

They crawled out into the open and stood up. The sun was low in the west, casting a rosy hue across the dunes on every side. A cool breeze stirred the leaves of the baobab tree and ruffled the surface of the sand. A chorus of animal sounds was starting up. Roosters crowed, donkeys brayed, guinea fowl squawked and jabbered.

The horses were quiet, apart from the occasional snort or whinny. Slingshot practice in the training ring had finished, but the horses stayed in the ring waiting patiently for their evening feed. Free of their bits and bridles, they stood right up close to the thorn-branch fence and watched with growing excitement while a young boy measured grain into a wide metal dish.

Jake and Kas wandered over to the smaller enclosure, where a wrestling match was taking place. Two muscular boys, stripped to the waist, were doing their best to trip each other up, and a dozen others were heckling or shouting advice. The boys circled each other like panthers and then clashed in wild flurries of dust and limbs. With them in the ring was some kind of referee wearing animal-tooth anklets that jangled as he walked.

"Watch the knees and elbows," said a voice in Jake's ear. It was Paaté, the tailor, now wearing a green floppy hat and a pair of spectacles with no lenses. "If a fighter's knees touch the ground, he loses. If his elbows touch the ground, he loses. One knee and one elbow, again he loses. But just one knee, or just one elbow, he can go on fighting."

"What if both his knees *and* both his elbows touch the ground?"

"That is a shameful way to lose," said Paaté. "If that happens, he will be washing his opponent's clothes for the next three months."

"Who is the best wrestler in the camp?"

"The Chameleon," said Paaté without hesitation. "No one has ever seen dust on the Chameleon's knees. He moves like an angel and he strikes like a djinn. Unbeatable."

Jake watched the shadows lengthen and fade as the sun went down over the western dunes. Somewhere in the camp a rifle fired. Kas jumped and looked around wildly.

"Do not be afraid," said Paaté. "That was the *nyiiri* rifle. It means the banquet is about to begin."

NINETEEN

The Red Cross marquee was lit by hurricane lamps and candles, and it smelled of tea leaves, mint, and roasted meat. The floor was covered with clean white sand, and a dozen straw mats were arranged in a semicircle. Paaté led Jake and Kas to an unoccupied mat. They kicked off their flip-flops and sat down. After that agonizing journey on horseback it still hurt to sit.

The marquee was filling up with hungry boys. There were a few girls, too, including Mariama. Only one person in the marquee was above the age of twenty—a plump thirty-something man with a short, pointed beard and two braided locks of hair hanging one on either side of his face. He was reclining on one elbow, eating dates from a silver dish and spitting out the stones.

Most of the boys wore three-quarter-length cotton robes

like Jake's, and they were talking excitedly among themselves, occasionally glancing across at the strange, sunburned visitors.

"Why is everyone talking French?" asked Jake.

Paaté shrugged. "The boys and girls here are from loads of different tribes, so French is the only language we all have in common."

Kas was scanning the rows of faces. "Where are Farm Eye and the others?" she asked. "I don't see them."

"Who?" asked Paaté.

"The boys who rescued us this morning."

"They left while you were sleeping. They live in Burizanga, between Djibo and Kongoussi. We work together on jobs sometimes."

"What kinds of jobs?"

Paaté ignored the question, and Kas did not press him further.

A little boy came around with a plastic bucket for hand washing, and two older boys followed behind, serving the food. Jake had expected another dose of *nyiiri*, but the crusty gray paste was nowhere to be seen. Instead, there was mint tea, soft black dates, succulent lamb roasted on the bone, bowls of cayenne pepper, and mountains of sticky white rice drenched in peanut sauce. The food could not have been more different from the prissy gourmet food of last night's gold banquet. Here the diners were holding their meat in their hands and tearing it with their teeth.

"Is the Chameleon here?" asked Kas, pulling a chunk of meat off a bone and dipping it in cayenne pepper.

"Be patient," said Paaté. "The Chameleon will be here presently." He snapped a bone between his fingers and sucked out the marrow.

Over the hubbub, a deep and resonant voice rang out. *"Allahu akbar! Allahu akbar!"* A disembodied head appeared at the front of the banqueting hall.

It was a young, dark face with a sardonic smile, and it floated in thin air about three feet above the ground. The unblinking eyes gazed around the hall, fixing the diners with an otherworldly stare. Kas gasped and clutched Jake's hand.

"Don't stress, Kas," whispered Jake. "It's some sort of trick—it has to be."

"It's the Chameleon," murmured Paaté. "He has arrived."

The head without a body turned from side to side. Then the mouth opened and began to speak. *"Salaam aleykum!"* said the Chameleon. *"Bonsoir à tout le monde."*

A few uncertain titters of laughter rippled around the hall. *"Aleykum asalaam!"* cried some.

Mirrors, thought Jake. *It has to be.* But there was no denying that the trick was well done and that the young illusionist had made an unforgettable entrance. Jake was impressed and at the same time a little afraid.

"I see our guest of honor is here," continued the French-speaking head, grinning at the bearded man who occupied the seat of honor. "Sheikh Ahmed, are you enjoying tonight's feast?"

The sheikh scowled and shook his head. "Who taught you my trick, you fiend?"

"The one who taught me is called Moussa," said the Chameleon. "I believe he used to be your disciple, Sheikh Ahmed."

As he spoke, a second disembodied head appeared beside his own.

The sheikh jumped to his feet, his cheeks and stomach quivering. "Moussa!" he cried, pointing an accusing finger at the second head. "How dare you disobey me! I told you to go to Senegal with my sheep and goats—"

"*Your* sheep and goats?" interrupted the Chameleon. "I thought they were for the djinns. I thought that Moussa was going to sacrifice those animals in Lake Soum in order to appease the djinns and release rain on Mondoro village."

"That's right," said the sheikh. "That was Moussa's task."

"It's a lie." This time it was Moussa's head that spoke.

"Sheikh Ahmed told me not to sacrifice the sheep and goats. He told me to take them to a faraway market and sell them. The whole thing was a ruse."

"A ruse?" cried the Chameleon, raising his eyebrows and pursing his lips comically.

"A ruse," said Moussa glumly.

The sheikh grabbed his walking stick, strode to the front of the hall, and swung it into the space beneath the floating heads. Two mirrors shattered into smithereens, and the floating heads gained bodies in an instant.

"Thank heaven I wore clothes today," murmured the Chameleon, getting up from his knees and flicking a speck of dust off his long-sleeved cotton robe. There was loud laughter from the assembly.

The sheikh strode in among the shattered glass and brandished his staff at the Chameleon. "Your impudence angers the djinns!" cried the sheikh, his beard quivering. "Tell me straight, trickster. Where are the animals you stole from me?"

The Chameleon bent down and picked up a rib that had been gnawed bare and discarded on the ground. "Here's one you ate earlier," he said.

Apoplectic with rage, the sheikh spat and cursed and swung

his staff, but the Chameleon anticipated the blow and dodged it neatly. Two boys jumped up and restrained the holy man, holding his arms while his fury dissipated.

"A group of our boys waylaid Moussa near the border," said the Chameleon. "He's a clever one, is Moussa. Fine nose for right and wrong."

"Traitor!" spat the sheikh, glaring at his former disciple.

"Look around you," cried the Chameleon, flinging wide his arms. "We are all traitors here. Each of us has chosen to turn his back on a dark master. Betrayal is the price of freedom. Moussa chose well, and your other servants too. As for you, Sheikh Ahmed, you will be leaving for Senegal first thing in the morning. I have already arranged transportation. If you ever set foot in Mali or Burkina Faso again, you will not escape so lightly."

Held tight between two muscular teenagers, the sheikh was escorted out of the marquee, his angry protestations fading into the night.

The Chameleon jumped high into the air and clicked his heels together. *"Hiila hiilataa bii nginnaawu!"* he cried. "Deceit cannot trick the son of a djinn!"

The boys cheered, and some of them threw flip-flops or bones into the air.

"We have not finished," said the Chameleon, skewering Jake and Kirsty with his gaze. "We have yet more guests to honor. Stand, friends, and tell us your names."

Jake got uneasily to his feet. "I'm Jake Knight," he said, "and this is my sister, Kirsty."

"*Ndawal nanndaa e pooli!*" cried the Chameleon. "Ostriches are not like other birds."

The audience cheered.

"These are no ordinary children," said the Chameleon, his voice sinking to a stage whisper. "We have among us the son and daughter of the King of England himself!"

"British ambassador," corrected Jake.

"They were kidnapped last night," continued the Chameleon. "They were kidnapped, the radio tells us, by a Saharan outlaw!"

"Which one?" cried a voice.

"By the most wicked outlaw ever to have lived," said the Chameleon. "A prince of the desert underworld, a master of disguise, a man who is full of compassion one minute and utterly heartless the next."

"Name him!"

"His name," said the Chameleon, "is Yakuuba Sor."

The marquee fell silent.

"How will the King of England respond to this atrocity?" asked the Chameleon. "He will rage, will he not? He will ransack the desert. He will find that outlaw's camp, and he will visit it with Death!"

Murmurs of consternation among the boys.

"One day," continued the Chameleon, "Yakuuba Sor will be sitting in his tent, and he will hear the sound of a skyboat. He will go outside and he will lift his gaze and he will wonder why that skyboat is flying so low. And that, my friends, will be the last thought he ever thinks, for Death will swiftly fall upon his head like mango rain from a clear sky." The Chameleon flung his arms dramatically into the air, and as he did so, the loose sleeves of his robe slid down to reveal his forearms.

Kas gasped.

Of course, thought Jake. *I should have guessed.*

Etched on the Chameleon's left forearm was a jet-black spiderweb tattoo.

Twenty

The Chameleon strode toward Jake and Kirsty and stopped in front of them. He folded his arms and stared at Jake as if he were looking right into his soul.

"You're him, aren't you?" said Jake. "You're Yakuuba Sor."

"*Enchanté*," said the Chameleon.

"You are the most wanted outlaw in all of Burkina Faso."

"And all of Mali, too."

"And these boys are the Friends of the Poor?"

"They are."

Jake turned to Kas. "When I say the word," he whispered in English, "we'll make a run for it. Just follow me and do what I do."

Kas nodded, too scared to speak.

"*Wanaa ko rawni fuu wo kosam,*" whispered Sor. "Not everything that is white is milk."

I must strike first, thought Jake. *Strike first and escape fast. No more dithering. Mungo Park escaped from the Moor because he saw his chance and grabbed it with both hands.*

"*Wanaa ko futini fuu wo yitere mbabatu,*" said Sor. "Not all protruding things are locust eyes."

In one swift movement, Jake reached down, picked up the bowl of cayenne pepper, and flung it in Sor's face. "Run!" he shouted, and he sprinted toward the back of the tent, with Kas close on his heels. When they got to the back of the marquee, they threw themselves to the ground and rolled under the canvas wall, out into the cool night air, into the camp lit by the silvery light of a half-moon.

"We're in the middle of the desert," wailed Kas. "There's nowhere to hide."

"We'll take a horse," said Jake, dashing toward the enclosure. He gathered up his robe as he ran and tucked it into his trousers. Out of the darkness behind them he heard voices shouting. Any moment now their pursuers would come swarming out of the marquee.

Jake swung open the five-bar gate to the horse enclosure. "You stand on the gate," he said, "and then jump on the horse as I come past."

"You'll need a bit and bridle," said Kas.

"There's no time to go looking for all that stuff," said Jake. "We'll just have to wing it."

A white stallion loomed in front of him. Jake approached him quickly and quietly. *Stay light on your toes,* thought Jake. *Don't startle him.* He shortened his stride as he got close to the stallion, tensing his body like a coiled spring. *Think of it as a straddle jump. Fluid and gentle.* He jumped off his right foot, placed his hands lightly on the horse's withers, and twisted his body in midair to bring his left leg up and over.

The white horse shied and reared when he felt the sudden weight land on his back. Jake kept his balance and kicked the horse's side as he had seen Farm Eye do. The stallion moved forward in a quick trot, heading for the gate with his ears flat back. Jake held out a hand to Kas, and she jumped across to join him on the horse's back.

The voices were louder now. Flashlight beams strobed to and fro. A small stone whizzed past Jake's head, stinging his cheek.

"They've spotted us," cried Jake. "Hang on tight!" He kicked hard with his heels, and his mount leaped forward. He put his head down, lengthened his stride, and cantered hard toward the domed huts.

"Nobody rides without reins!" said Kas. "It's madness!

We have absolutely no way of controlling which direction he goes in."

"I don't care which direction he goes in," said Jake, "so long as he goes fast." He kicked again, and the horse moved up another gear into a full-blown gallop.

They flew past the domed straw huts, veering east toward the dunes. Jake threw his arms around the stallion's neck and clung on with all his strength. Behind him, Kas locked her arms so tight around his chest that he could hardly breathe. They did not need to look behind them, for the thud of pursuing hooves was unmistakable.

The chase did not last long. The white stallion balked at the foot of the nearest dune and sent Jake and Kirsty flying over his head.

Jake shielded his head with his arms and rolled to a standstill. There was no time to make a run for it. Sor was already upon them, glaring down at them from the seat of his horse. Paaté was not far behind.

"Kuldo bolli si yi'ii loosol fu doggan!" cried Sor. "He who fears snakes will flee from a stick. Tell me, *tuubaakus*, are you hurt?"

"No," said Jake.

"Why did you run?"

"Because you are a dangerous outlaw."

"Nowru walaa omboode," said Sor. "The ear does not have a lid. What you say is true, *tuubaaku*. I am extremely dangerous. Last night I poisoned twelve grain merchants, and today I removed thirty-five bicycles from a police compound and humiliated a celebrity sheikh. But it is not enough for you to ask, *Is Yakuuba Sor dangerous?* You should instead ask: *Is Yakuuba Sor dangerous* to me? And in your case, the answer is no."

"You don't want to hurt us?"

Yakuuba Sor chuckled. "Believe me when I say that you are more dangerous to me than I am to you. When I heard on the radio that I was wanted for kidnapping two *tuubaaku* children, the terror of it sliced my liver clean down the middle."

"Why?"

"Because your people strike first and ask questions later, as you just proved."

Jake felt a fleeting pang of guilt. "All we want is to go home," he said.

"In my experience," said Yakuuba, "home is usually the very last place a young person wants to go. But as it happens, this is a matter on which our interests coincide. I want you to go home, as well. First, there is something I need to know. Why does the radio believe that I was responsible for your kidnapping?"

"We phoned my father from inside the van," said Jake. "We told him that we had seen a spiderweb tattoo on our kidnapper's left arm."

"*Allah wallu en.*" Yakuuba shook his head. "Heaven help us."

"We realized later that the tattoo wasn't real."

"Not real?" said Yakuuba. "And what do you think about that?"

"We don't know what to think."

"Nonsense! There are only three kinds of people who do not know what to think—the very old, the very young, and the very feverish—and I see from your skin that you are none of those. So tell me, what do you think?"

"Someone was pretending to be you," said Jake.

"Who?"

"How should we know? Do you have any enemies?"

Sor threw back his head and laughed like a hyena. "Do you see the stars above your head, *tuubaaku?* That is how many enemies I have."

"Well, then," said Jake, "if one of your enemies can make

our people believe that you have kidnapped and killed us, our government will not rest until they have destroyed you."

Yakuuba Sor nodded. "We are all in very great danger," he said. "Paaté, go to the Needle Hut and start work. Our guests will need proper disguises—the best you have ever made!"

Twenty-one

Yakuuba's plan was very simple. They would ride in disguise to Djibo and take the bus from there to Ouagadougou. Once there, Yakuuba would escort Jake and Kas to the embassy. With their help he would explain to their father that the Friends of the Poor were innocent of the kidnapping and that he, Yakuuba Sor, had no quarrel with the British.

"We have a long journey ahead of us," said Yakuuba, "so get some sleep. I will wake you before sunrise for the ride to Djibo."

Getting some sleep was easier said than done. When they got back to their hut, Jake and Kas were still buzzing with adrenaline from their attempted escape and at the same time dreading what the next day might have in store for them. How, wondered Jake, had they gotten caught up in this power play between a young outlaw and his enemies?

After an hour or two, Jake drifted into fretful sleep. He dreamed he was riding a black horse, which suddenly sprouted wings and soared up over the desert in an exhilarating but terrifying climb. He flew over djinns, dunes, camels, wadis, and a whole convoy of menacing Nissan vans.

"Réveillez-vous," said a voice. "Wake up and come with me."

Jake opened his eyes and saw a man crouching at the foot of his bed. Right away he recognized the goatee beard and the two dangling locks of hair that framed the intruder's face. It was none other than Sheikh Ahmed. The sheikh had changed into a green robe with intricate embroidery down the front, and he wore a pair of dark glasses, unusual for this hour of the morning.

"I thought they took you away," stammered Jake.

"They did," said the sheikh. "And now I am back, to help you with your *maquillage.*"

"What is *maquillage?*"

"Makeup," said Kas, sitting up. "And you may have fooled my brother, Yakuuba, but you can't fool me. Your stomach's hanging off."

Yakuuba Sor chuckled and adjusted the cords around his waist. "Come with me," he said. "Your makeup awaits you."

The sun had not yet risen, but a swath of gray and indigo in the eastern sky indicated that the night was nearly past. Jake and Kas crawled out into the invigorating morning air and shook hands with Yakuuba. The stubby upward-pointing branches of the baobab tree loomed above them like the crenellations of a wizard's castle.

Paaté and Mariama were waiting for them in the Needle Hut, where two sets of fine clothes hung from a ceiling beam. The workbench was covered with lotions and potions.

Yakuuba lifted up one end of a rickety wooden bench so that its cargo of cotton, scissors, plastic bags, clothes hangers, foam, sequins, and zippers slid off onto the floor. "Sit down," he said to Kas, "and listen carefully. Your name is Kadija Zabri and you are a Tuareg princess from the Niger delta. You are traveling to Ouagadougou with your personal praise singer, Bobo Nuhu, played by Paaté here. Also traveling with you is Sheikh Ahmed Abdullai Keita and your idiot brother Ali."

"Hey!" cried Jake.

"I'm sorry, Ali," said Yakuuba, "but your French accent is terrible. You will attract less attention if you simply gibber in some made-up language of your own."

"I've never gibbered in my life," said Jake. "I wouldn't know how. And you can shut up laughing, Kas."

"You don't need to gibber," said Yakuuba. "Just don't talk at all, if you would prefer that."

"Why Tuaregs?" asked Kas.

"Tuareg nobles have long noses," said Mariama, "and their skin is lighter than other Africans."

"As light as my skin?"

"Of course not," said Mariama. "In this part of Africa, only djinns are as pale as you are. But don't worry. We have a tub of moringa pulp here somewhere. By sunrise you will both look more Tuareg than *tuubaaku*, I promise you."

Sure enough, over the course of the next hour the children of the British ambassador were transformed. Paaté shaved Jake's head bald and plastered moringa pulp over his whole head and face, even on his eyelids and the insides of his ears. In addition to its skin-darkening effect, the pulp felt cool and soothing across his sunburned nose and cheeks. He was sorry when the time came for it to be washed off.

When he was able to open his eyes, Jake saw that his sister was well on the way to becoming a Tuareg princess. Her skin was a shade darker and her earlobes were decorated with rows of tiny silver rings. Her hair, parted down the middle, was woven through with silver coins and amber beads all the way from

Mali. Three short black lines adorned her cheekbones, lending her the untouchable air of a warrior queen.

"How do I look?" she said.

"Scary," said Jake. "What about me?"

"Undead."

The clothes were exquisite. Kas got a long indigo dress, lavishly embellished with white braid. Across the top of her head she wore a black shawl inlaid with strips of silver. Jake got a pair of baggy green trousers, a blue turban, and a white robe that reached all the way down to his knees. For Paaté there was an orange cassock and a floppy black and white beret.

"Almost there," said Yakuuba Sor. "Somebody fetch Princess Kadija an amber ring and an armful of silver bracelets. Paaté, you will need a three-stringed lute. And give Ali a sword. No self-respecting Tuareg prince would walk unarmed in a town like Djibo."

By the time the sun rose over the camp, the disguises were complete. Outside the door of the Needle Hut came a loud whinny of anticipation.

"Time to ride!" declared Yakuuba.

The three horses waiting outside the Needle Hut were dressed to impress. They wore fine yellow saddles, embroidered

red and black saddle cloths, tasseled reins, and tough goatskin stirrup leathers.

Yakuuba had chosen to ride Sheikh Ahmed's white stallion and to entrust his own horse, Silalé, to Paaté and Jake. Silalé was a black stallion with a proud head and a long arching neck. A white blaze graced his forehead and steel muscles rippled under his glossy flanks. He flattened his ears at Jake's approach and gave an angry snort.

"Mount from the left, not the right!" cried Kas. "And talk to him, tell him who you are."

Jake climbed into the saddle, and Paaté hopped on behind. Kas and Mariama were also sharing a horse, a beautiful mare with a light tan hide, black mane, and black tail.

"We're going to have to blindfold you to start with," said Paaté, "but after that we'll let you take control."

The blindfolds went on and the horses took off. Once again, Jake felt a jolt of fear and a strange lightness in his tummy.

"I've seen sacks of millet flour sit better than you!" cried Paaté behind him. "Use the stirrups!"

It was disorienting trying to ride blind, but eventually Jake found a rhythm. He learned to put his weight on the stirrups as Silalé's shoulders swung down, and to rise slightly in the saddle when the shoulders rose again.

Paaté was as good as his word. After twenty minutes of trotting and walking he let Jake remove the blindfold and take the reins himself. "Put your hands like this," he said. "Imagine you are holding two goblets of Mariama's mango wine."

Jake kept a light pressure on Silalé's mouth and trotted gently, rising and falling with the stallion's gait. Over the crest of a dune they went, and down onto a great plain that stretched as far as the eye could see. *Beogo was right about the danger,* thought Jake. *This vast flat arena would be a great location for an apocalypse.*

Silalé must have felt it too, because he was throwing his head from side to side and champing on his bit. Jake glanced at Kas and Mariama. He saw Kas relax her grip on the reins and give the horse its head, and immediately the mare shot off across the plain with a beautiful racing stride. The mare was like the bottom of a wave, pitching violently to and fro, with Kas and Mariama as the quiet crest. Smooth and elegant, they ebbed and flowed, indigo dresses flying in their wake.

"Mo buraa maa yahde fuu taa bure collaare," Yakuuba shouted to Jake. "If someone is slower than you, don't let them make more dust than you."

"What do you mean?"

"Silalé is a matchless creature, the fastest horse in the Sahara. Are you really going to let your sister and Mariama beat you on that old nag?"

Jake summoned his courage and spurred the stallion into a fierce gallop. Silalé sprang forward, his great spirit finally unleashed. As he accelerated, the plain slid away beneath them in a dizzying blur, dry earth crackling under the pounding of his hooves. Camel grass flashed by. Spume flakes flew from Silalé's mouth. Paaté whooped and punched the air. Already they were gaining on the girls.

Jake was no jockey. All he could do was hold on tight to the front piece of the saddle and roll with the savage motion of the horse. Desert wind blew hot against his face. Intoxicating power and joy raged beneath him.

Neck and neck, stride by stride the horses lunged forward, with first one and then another surging ahead. A Tuareg prince and princess, a celebrity sheikh, and a minstrel—galloping together, they made a very impressive traveling party. The three steeds ran to the limit of their energy and then at last slowed down, staggering, heavy, and dripping with sweat.

"Djibo straight ahead," said Paaté. "Look, there's the phone tower."

Jake strained his eyes and was just able to make out the

slender tower. He took his phone from his money belt, and sure enough, there was one bar of network coverage, then two, then three.

"Kas!" he cried. "I've got a signal!" He took both reins in his right hand and used his left to dial the embassy. Dad was a morning person and was sure to be up by now. In fact, he was probably finding it difficult to sleep at all. Sure enough, Mr. Knight answered the phone after only one ring.

"Dad!" cried Jake. "It's me."

The white stallion came cantering up, and Yakuuba snatched the phone out of his hand. "No phone calls," said the outlaw. "I have learned not to trust telephones."

"That was my father," said Jake. "I was going to let him know what's happening. I was going to tell him that you were not responsible for our kidnapping."

"He would not have believed you," said Yakuuba. "This afternoon I will meet your father face to face, and then he will believe."

TWENTY-TWO

"Dexter!" Mr. Knight knocked on the door of the spare room. "Wake up! Wake up, I tell you."

Dexter opened the door in his boxer shorts. He was bleary-eyed and his face was framed by greasy curls. Mr. Knight was shocked to see there were three cruel diagonal scars across his chest.

"What do you want?" said Dexter.

"I'm sorry," said the ambassador. "I didn't mean to stare. But are those—?"

"Turkmenistan, yes. And I have learned my lesson."

"Jake phoned."

"What did he say?"

"Nothing. Sor must have taken the phone off him."

"Pity." The MI6 officer yawned and rubbed his unshaven chin.

"The point is, Dexter, the phone is back in range of a tower. We have a fix."

"Excellent." There it was again, that gleam of fear in the man's eyes.

"I have already told Commissioner Beogo the news," said Mr. Knight. "He is sending a driver to pick you up."

Dexter darted back into his room, grabbed his beetle tin, and opened the lid a fraction. "Xena, my beauty, we have a fix, which means your time has come. Today you will assist in the disincentivization of Yakuuba Sor."

"That is secondary," said Mr. Knight. "Your primary objective, remember, is the rescue of my children."

"Rescue," murmured Dexter. "Of course."

A horn sounded outside the gate.

"There's your driver," said Mr. Knight. "I suggest you put some clothes on."

Twenty-Three

Near**ly** there!" shouted Paaté.

"Faster!" cried Yakuuba Sor. "There is only one bus every day, and we must not miss it!"

Jake spurred his horse and led the charge along a sandy track. On either side the fields flashed by, interspersed with clusters of dome-shaped dwellings. The sun shone on Jake's face and the air blew deep into his lungs, but he was still angry about his phone. How dare Yakuuba snatch it off him like that? What was so bad about letting Dad know they were on their way home?

The more Jake thought about it, the less he trusted Sor. Even if he was not a kidnapper, he was still an outlaw. *Outlaws are thieves and murderers, and there is not a speck of cool in any of them.*

In front of them loomed a metal water tower and a WELCOME TO DJIBO sign. Beyond that a vast herd of cows milled about.

"Customs post," said Yakuuba, slowing to a trot. "They're counting cows."

"Why?"

"There is a government tax on all movement of livestock. Yesterday was market day, when rich traders come to Djibo to buy cows. Today those rich traders will employ poor cattle herders to walk the cows to Ouagadougou."

"They walk all the way from here to Ouaga? How long does that take?"

"Eight days," said Yakuuba. "I should know—I used to do it for a living. Every alternate Thursday I'd be right here at the cow count, waiting to set off on another one-hundred-fifty-mile walk."

Jake looked at the cows with their crescent horns, humped backs, and scrawny rib cages. They were sickly specimens, and he wondered how many of them would survive the journey to Ouagadougou.

The closer they got to the marketplace at the center of the town, the busier the streets became. Camels lurched past carrying piles of straw mats and other wares. Women sat outside their houses selling milk or *nyiiri* or fried millet pancakes. A gaggle of small children ran alongside the horses shouting, *"Cadeau, cadeau!"* Sor threw a handful of coins, which the children gathered up, shrieking and giggling.

"There's the bus station," said Paaté, pointing along the central market street to a sign bearing the letters STMB. "Société Transport Mamadou Bagadumba, the most punctual bus company in the country."

A crowd of people was converging on the bus station. Some rode pillion on motorbikes, holding their traveling bags above their heads. Others rode makeshift wooden carts pulled by donkeys. Still others hurried along on foot.

The bus was already there. The STMB lettering across the side of the bus was chipped and faded, and the gaping window frames were without glass. Two mechanics tinkered and squabbled beneath the raised hood. This did not look like a bus that was going anywhere soon.

A rickety scaffold had been erected next to the vehicle. Three young porters were balancing on top of the scaffold, taking people's luggage from ground level and hoisting it up to their colleagues on the bus roof. The porters wore blue STMB overalls and baseball caps. Their biceps shone with perspiration as they worked.

Yakuuba and his companions dismounted. Paaté threw the reins over Silalé's head and looped them through a metal ring in the wall of the bus station. The stallion snorted and twisted his head to nuzzle Jake's palm.

Two beggar boys ran up to Yakuuba and bowed so low, their noses almost touched the ground. They were identical twins with shaved heads, big eyes, and protruding front teeth.

"Hassan and Husseyni," whispered Mariama. "President and vice-president of our Friends of the Poor Djibo cell."

"Which is which?"

"I'm not sure, but they're both very loyal. They have agreed to ride the horses back to the camp with me."

"You mean you're not coming with us?"

"Buses make me sick," said Mariama, climbing back onto her horse, "and Ouagadougou makes me lonely. *Bon voyage, tuubaakus.*"

They said their goodbyes to Mariama and watched the horses depart. Then they joined the line, or rather the throng, at the ticket office.

"When does the bus leave?" asked Kas, eyeing it with suspicion.

"In principle," said Paaté, "fifteen minutes ago."

"I thought you said STMB was punctual," said Jake.

"Shut up, Ali," hissed Paaté. "You're not supposed to be talking. And all I said was that STMB is the most punctual bus company in the country. The others are even worse, I promise you."

Kas was starting to draw curious looks. Her indigo dress and silver-threaded shawl were out of keeping with the squalor of the bus station.

"They are wondering where you are from," said Paaté. "I'm going to have to say something." He shrugged his three-stringed lute off his shoulder and began to tune it. "Greatness must be honored!" he yelled. "People of the bus, lend me your ears. Genealogy burns in my bones; I must speak and find relief."

As the crowd pressed around him, Paaté fingerpicked an elaborate arpeggio, tapped the body of his lute three times, and began to chant: "Her name is Kadija Zabri, her name is Princess Zabri, Kadija the fair, Kadija the discreet, her name is Kadija Zabri. Loving daughter to Zabri Mannga, Sammba Mannga, Saalu Mannga, Booyi Mannga, Amnatu Mannga, Kumbo Mannga, Jeneba Mannga, an honorable generation. Mannga Haamidi, Mamadou Haamidi, a lofty generation. Haamidi Alu, Iisaa Alu, Buguuru Alu, Fajaaji Alu, Atiko Alu, Abdusalam Alu, Sekeeru Alu, Salaamata Alu, Djiika Alu, a pious generation.

Alu Oumarou, Galo Oumarou, I'm halfway there already. Do you hear me, people of the bus?"

"We hear you!" cried a voice.

"Get on with it!" cried another.

"Oumarou Ba Samba, Hama Ba Samba, Maaliki Ba Samba, Bure Ba Samba, Alu Ba Samba, an honorable generation. Ba Samba Nyorgo, Hamadum Nyorgo, Hamadi Njaare Nyorgo, Bura Nyorgo, Buubu Nyorgo, Oumarou Nyorgo, a lofty generation. Nyorgo Mbuula, Mbabba Mbuula, Belko Mbuula, Paaté Mbuula, a pious generation. Mbuula Ali, Mboldi Ali, sons of Ali Simbi Ko'e, the first of the Tuareg Maasina, an honorable, lofty, pious forefather indeed!"

There was some nodding and clapping and a few cries of "Welcome to Djibo, Princess Zabri!"

Kas patted the amber beads in her hair and smiled back graciously.

"What about me?" whispered Jake. "I'm new in town as well."

"They don't seem so interested in you," said Paaté. "Take your tickets, my friends—it's time to climb aboard!"

The hood of the bus was lowered, the man with the wrenches slid out from the vehicle's underbelly, and the passenger door stood open. The travelers surged at once toward the open door, waving their tickets above their heads.

"Come on, your highnesses!" cried Yakuuba. "If you hang back now, you'll be standing all the way to Ouaga!"

Jake and Kas waded into the fray and were carried toward the bus by the eager tide. The crowd at the door formed a bone-crushing bottleneck, but Paaté's cries of "Make way for the princess" seemed to ease their passage. A minute later they were on the bus. They managed to get the last available seats, four seats together along the very back row.

"We will feel all the bumps, sitting back here," said Yakuuba, "but at least no one will bother us. Try to make yourself comfortable, if you can."

Even after the last seats were taken, the bus continued to fill up. Passengers stood shoulder to shoulder all the way along the aisle. They bickered and gossiped and stowed their bags and chickens in the overhead luggage racks.

The engine spluttered into life and the horn blared to signal imminent departure. The interior of the bus was hot and stuffy in spite of the open windows, and exhaust fumes seemed to be leaking in under the seats.

"I don't feel too great," said Jake. "I think I'm going to throw up."

"Serves you right for guzzling all that dirty well water yesterday," said Kas. "Don't worry," she added. "A few hours from now we'll be back at home and you can be as ill as you want. You can lie in bed all day tomorrow drinking chicken noodle soup."

The porters who had been tying luggage onto the roof rack now swung themselves down from the roof and in through the empty window frames. Street peddlers outside were also making the most of the vehicle's lack of windows. They offered up their wares on enormous oval plates: hunks of grilled fish, cobs of corn, sesame-seed biscuits, bananas—all sorts of tempting delicacies jostled for position. Clusters of *garibous*—quranic students—congregated at the windows. They brandished their begging bowls and yelled shrill blessings at the passengers.

Paaté tossed the boys a handful of coins. "I used to be a *garibou* myself," he said. "Besides, this journey of ours needs all the blessings it can get."

There was a stir at the front of the bus. People were rising from their seats and craning their necks to look. A man in uniform had gotten on the bus. It was a *gendarme*, a member of Burkina Faso's military police.

The policeman said a few words to the bus driver and turned to glare at the passengers. *"Cartes d'identité!"* he cried.

"Heaven help us," muttered Paaté. "It's an identity check."

"Is that normal?" asked Jake.

"Five years ago, yes, but these days they only do it if they're looking for someone in particular."

"Who do you think they're looking for?"

"Isn't it obvious?"

"Fine," said Jake, rising from his seat. "We'll just have to tell him who we are."

Yakuuba shoved him back into his seat with a firm hand. "Never tell the truth to a man in uniform," he said.

The *gendarme* was making his way slowly up the aisle, elbowing past the standing peasants and checking identity cards as he went. He stopped to remonstrate with an old woman in the aisle. She did not have an identity card, neither did she speak French. The *gendarme* tutted and scowled and pushed the woman aside. He had a pistol in his belt.

Kas seemed to be having some trouble breathing. She had paled under her moringa-pulp tan, and her lower lip was trembling.

"What is it?" whispered Jake.

"It's him," Kas said. *"It's the waiter."*

Twenty-Four

The *gendarme* was now no more than ten feet away. He was a thirty-something man wearing a camouflage uniform, a green beret, and black ankle-high boots. He had tired, bloodshot eyes and a slight swelling on his right temple. Jake's eye wandered again to those black boots. He had seen boots like that before. Keep your eyes lowered, their father had told them. *Lowered eyes meant ample opportunity to study boots.*

"It can't be," whispered Jake. "Same boots, for sure, but that doesn't necessarily mean—"

"Look at that lump above his eye," said Kas. "Don't you remember, Jake, he got hit by a stone when those boys rescued us. I'm telling you, it's him."

Yakuuba wagged his index finger in front of her face. "Stop talking *tuubaaku* language," he hissed. "You are a Tuareg princess, remember?"

"But Yakuuba, this is important," whispered Kas. *"That's one of the men who kidnapped us."*

The *gendarme* was now only two rows from the back of the bus and heading inexorably their way. Jake clenched his teeth hard to stop them from chattering. His sister was right; it was definitely their kidnapper. Up close, even the sickly smell of his aftershave was familiar.

The Chameleon stood up. He moved down the aisle and tried to squeeze past the *gendarme*.

"Carte d'identité," snapped the gendarme, holding out a stiff arm to block his way.

Yakuuba took out his identity card and handed it over.

The name on the card provoked quite a reaction. The *gendarme* gave an audible gasp, and his hand went straight to the gun in his belt. Quick as a flash, Sor seized the policeman's collar, put a foot behind his leg, and flipped him over onto the floor of the bus. The throw Jake had just witnessed was real wrestling magic: sudden, powerful, and perfectly controlled. *No one has ever seen dust on the Chameleon's knees.*

The Chameleon did not hang around to chat with his opponent. He snatched back the identity card, grabbed the lip of the overhead luggage compartment, swung himself feet first through the empty window frame, and landed on the forecourt of the bus station. The onlookers marveled to see an overweight sheikh display such grace and agility.

The *gendarme* was quick to react. As he got up from the floor, he drew his pistol from its holster and flicked the safety catch off. With his other hand he grabbed the whistle around his neck and blew it hard and shrill. Then he launched himself out of the window in pursuit of the outlaw.

Jake stood up and craned his neck to watch the chase unfold. The Chameleon was heading toward the gates of the bus station, and it seemed very likely that he would get away, but just as he neared the gates, he was met by two more *gendarmes* coming in, summoned no doubt by their colleague's frantic whistle blowing. The Chameleon skidded to a halt in a cloud of dust, turned around, and sprinted back across the forecourt.

"Couchez-vous tous par terre!" cried the whistle blower. "Everybody get down!"

Everyone except the Chameleon threw themselves into the dust. The *gendarme* trained his pistol at the Chameleon's head and pulled the trigger. A chunk of concrete dropped out of the wall behind the fleeing outlaw. The *gendarme* swore and took aim at the larger target of Sor's body, and this time he did not miss. Sor dropped to the ground and lay there motionless.

Jake and Kas stared in disbelief. Paaté clapped a hand to his mouth. *"Allahu akbar,"* he said. "It is not possible."

A hue and cry went up from the passengers on the bus and from those on the forecourt. Peddlers, porters, and donkey cart owners rushed forward and formed a tight huddle around the outlaw's body, pointing at the bullet hole and shaking their heads in shock. Men who died like this at the hands of the police were usually thieves, but this man did not look like a thief. If anything he looked like a sheikh.

The *gendarme* blew on the barrel of his pistol, replaced it in its holster, and swaggered toward the crowd, swinging his shoulders like a small-town sheriff. "Get away from that body!" he shouted. "Stand clear, I tell you!"

"I know this sheikh," muttered a local grain merchant. "I met him the other night at the home of Al Hajji Amadou. His name is Sheikh Ahmed Abdullai Keita, and he performs miracles that would make your eyes spin in their sockets."

"The police have murdered a holy man!" cried an old woman.

"An evil day indeed!" moaned another.

"Get away from there," said the *gendarme*, reaching the edge of the crowd. "Stand aside and let me through."

"Woe is us!"

"Misery me!"

"The sheikh is dead and so are we!"

"Wait! Look at that!"

"He's moving!"

"Allahu akbar!"

"He's getting up!"

"He's taking off his stomach!"

"It's another miracle!"

The *gendarme* gave a bloodcurdling roar and barged his way through to the center of the crowd. When he got there, the Chameleon's body was nowhere to be seen. All that was left was a stomach-shaped cushion with a bullet entry hole in one side and an exit hole in the other.

"Where is he?" snapped the *gendarme*. "Which way did he go?"

"Over there," said the grain merchant, pointing to a towering pyramid of millet sacks. "He ran and hid in there, behind my grain."

The *gendarme* sprinted over to the pyramid and squeezed in

behind the millet sacks. There was nobody there. He dashed out the other side and ran into a young porter wearing blue STMB overalls and a baseball cap.

"Did you see the sheikh?" gasped the *gendarme*, grabbing the porter by his lapels.

"Was he wearing green robes?" said the porter.

"Yes."

"Little pointy beard? Dangly hair?"

"Exactly. Where did he go?"

"Up there," said the porter, pointing into the branches of a mango tree that overhung the wall of the bus station.

"Quick," said the *gendarme*. "Give me a leg up."

The porter obliged. He interlaced his fingers and hoisted the policeman up into the branches of the tree. The crowd puffed out their cheeks, pointed up into the tree, and chattered.

Back in the bus, Paaté wiped his eyes with his sleeve. "Good," he said. "The danger is past."

"Speak for yourself," said Kas. "If Yakuuba is in that tree, then his danger is totally *not* past."

"Yakuuba is not in that tree."

"Where is he then?"

Paaté pointed at the porter in the blue STMB overalls, who

was now strolling away from the mango tree, chewing on a bent twig. As he passed their window, the porter looked up and winked at them. Jake nearly laughed out loud.

"That's why we call Yakuuba the Chameleon," said Paaté. "He can change his whole disguise quicker than most people can change their socks."

Kas stared. "You mean he was carrying those STMB clothes all the time?"

"He was wearing them," said Paaté. "The Chameleon always says that one disguise is never enough. If you want to stay safe, you should wear one disguise over another."

"Amazing," said Kas.

The three *gendarmes* searched the bus station for the resurrected outlaw. They drew ugly-looking knives from their ankle holsters and proceeded to stab and slash at every millet sack and traveling bag in sight.

"It's only a matter of time until they search the bus again," said Paaté. "We need to get out of here."

"And go where?" said Kas. "I thought this was the only bus to Ouaga."

"It is. And we're safer on it than in it." So saying, Paaté hauled himself onto the window frame and reached up to grab the edge of the roof rack above. His legs dangled briefly and then disappeared.

Jake followed him; then it was Kas's turn. She let herself be hoisted up onto the roof like a sack of potatoes. No one in the bus saw them go—everyone was too busy staring out the windows at the antics of the three furious *gendarmes.*

The roof of the bus was piled high with motorbikes, sacks of grain, caged chickens, and travel bags. Paaté burrowed into the middle of the luggage, loosening a knot here and heaving a millet sack there until he had hollowed out a comfortable den for the three of them.

"No one will see us in here," he said. "Except the chickens in that cage, and they can't tell anybody."

There followed an agonizing half hour of waiting. Jake and Kas held their breath as they listened to the *gendarmes* moving around inside the bus, barking orders and insults. The *gendarmes* checked and rechecked the passengers, but not one of them thought to search the luggage on the roof.

At long last the search was abandoned. The horn of the bus proclaimed its departure, and the engine grumbled into life. The bus edged out of the station, navigating what seemed to be an impossibly tight space between two buildings. A figure in blue overalls, crouched on the tin roof of one of the buildings, stood up and leaped across onto the roof rack of the bus, rolled silently over the piles of luggage, and tumbled down into Paaté's makeshift den.

"*Salaam aleykum,*" whispered the Chameleon. "Peace be upon you."

"*Aleykum asalaam,*" chorused Paaté, Jake, and Kas.

"Paaté, I do believe your eyes are red," said the Chameleon. "Don't tell me you cried!"

"Of course I cried," said Paaté. "That robe is only three days old and already you have riddled it with bullet holes."

Twenty-Five

The bus drove south past the mosque, the hospital, the military barracks, and the orphanage. On the outskirts of the town was a magnificent whitewashed villa set in private gardens, and from his vantage point on top of the bus, Jake could see over the high security wall into the gardens. There were bougainvillea vines all around the lawn, and a stone fountain in the middle gushed good clean water. Two ostriches stood at the fountain, arching their necks to drink.

"That house belongs to the mayor of Djibo," said Paaté. "One time, when he was away on business, I got into his garden with some lads from the Djibo cell, and we had an ostrich race across the lawn. You would be surprised how tricky it is to ride a sprinting ostrich."

As the bus traveled south out of town, the concrete houses

became mud-brick dwellings, which in turn became straw huts and goatskin tents. Finally all signs of human habitation disappeared. On both sides of the road the flat scrubland stretched away to a shimmering horizon.

"One hundred fifty miles to Ouagadougou," said Yakuuba. "It will take us about five hours, *inshallah*, if you include all the stopping and starting."

Jake leaned back against a sack of millet and gazed out at the sideways-scrolling savannah. It felt good to be going home, but he was still no closer to understanding the events of the last two days. Most confusing of all was the discovery that at least one of their kidnappers was a *gendarme*, a member of the military police.

"Why would a policeman want to kidnap us?" he asked out loud. "It does not make any sense."

"*Au contraire*," said Yakuuba, "it makes perfect sense. You yourselves said that someone was trying to frame me, to provoke your people into hunting me down. I have many enemies, Jake, but none more bitter or more powerful than the police."

"Why do they hate you so much?"

Yakuuba took a cola nut from his top pocket and bit into it. "Let me explain," he said. "Policemen in our country do not earn a big salary, so they supplement their pay with little extras. They accept bribes from the rich, they extort money from the poor, and they impose irregular 'taxes' or 'fines' on anyone too simple to stand up for his rights. Some are more corrupt, some are less corrupt, but none is ever held accountable for his actions. Have you ever seen a *gendarme* with a name tag on his lapel?"

"No."

"Neither have I. And yet the law of the land states that a *gendarme* should wear his name tag at all times. Power without accountability, Jake. That is the reason our country is sick. And that is why the poor need protecting. Take yesterday, for example. On Wednesdays, as you know, villagers from all over the province come to Djibo market. Yesterday morning, everybody entering the town with a bicycle was stopped by the police and asked to show paperwork to prove their bike was theirs. Those who were not able to show a valid receipt right then and there had their bicycles impounded by the police, pending payment of a twenty-thousand-franc fine, which is five times the official fine."

"That's not fair."

"That's what we thought. At about midday we gathered the

Djibo cell and went to the police compound. We removed all thirty-five bikes and gave them back to their owners."

"Was there a fight?"

"Not even a scuffle. Cunning is better than force, Jake. The hero of most African folktales is not the lion or the bear, but the rabbit."

"I see," said Jake. "And do you often pull stunts like that?"

"All the time. Not long ago the local magistrate, Judge Jiabaté, had Widow Wolof's mud-brick hut bulldozed to make way for his new Palace of Justice. We asked everybody in Djibo to donate one brick, and we built her a mansion."

"Nice."

"And when we heard that a foreign gold-mining company was polluting Djibo Lake, we dressed up as water sprites and haunted their mine."

"And just last week," broke in Paaté, "when the mayor announced a new livestock tax, we organized cacophonies in the road outside his villa."

"What are cacophonies?"

"Loud nighttime livestock parties, where everybody brings either a rooster, a dog, or a donkey!"

Jake laughed. "I'm not surprised the authorities hate you,"

he said. "What gives you the right to do all this? Who appointed you to the role of Chief Protector of the Poor?"

"Our people have a proverb," said Yakuuba. "*Allah reenata baali, amma Allah wi'ii, sannaa baali ngadanee hoggo.* It is God who protects sheep from the wolf, but God also says that sheep should have an enclosure made for them."

"Meaning?"

"We all have a part to play. It is our duty to protect the poor from the bad habits of the rich."

Jake nodded. It was impossible not to admire this crazy young vigilante and his gang. He thought about his own schooldays in England, and all of a sudden his life seemed very empty and selfish. Friends and apps were the only two things he really cared about.

"What about that sheikh back at the camp?" asked Kas. "What's his story?"

"He was one of our special projects," said Yakuuba. "When someone is exploiting the poor in a particularly nasty way, we bring them back to the camp and we try to show them the error of their ways. Sheikh Ahmed used to tour villages making promises of rain in exchange for sheep and goats. Somebody had to stop him."

Jake glanced at the wicker cage opposite, and even the chickens seemed to be glaring at him accusingly. *You call yourself an adventurer, Jake Knight, but what good has your adventuring ever done? Has geothimble ever made a difference to injustice or poverty or pollution? Has wall running ever provided a widow with a house to live in? You're not an adventurer, Knight, you're a consumer. Mr. Joyce was right all along. Too much technology and too little moral fiber.*

"I still don't understand," said Jake. "Dad hinted that the Friends of the Poor were an African branch of some international terrorist organization."

"Did he, really? And who told him that, I wonder?"

"Beogo."

Yakuuba looked up sharply. "*Haut Commissaire* François Beogo? The police commissioner in Ouagadougou? Does your father know him?"

"We all do. He sat with us at a banquet the night we got kidnapped."

"How interesting," said Yakuuba. "I have known Commissioner Beogo a long time. He seems to have made it his life's mission to destroy me."

"How come?"

"Last year Paaté and I borrowed the Djibo police van without asking. We were using it to transport grain and milk powder to a group of Tuareg refugees near Naasumba. They had no food, so it seemed the right thing to do, but the police lieutenant in Djibo did not see it that way. When he found out who had taken his van, he got very upset and he called in FIMO to find our camp and destroy it. FIMO, Force d'Intervention Militaire de Ouagadougou, is a branch of special forces, and at the time François Beogo was their commander. They came up to the north and spent months on end hunting for our camp."

"They made life impossible for us," said Paaté. "They were very good trackers, much better than the local police, and we had some very narrow escapes. Six times we had to move our camp to a new location. In the end, Yakuuba decided that something had to be done, so he sent a message to Beogo challenging him to a calabar duel."

"What's that?"

"A calabar duel is the method our ancestors used for resolving arguments. Archenemies meet in the bush next to a calabar tree, and each of them picks a calabar bean from the tree. Calabar beans are poisonous, you see. They say a prayer, and then both men swallow their beans at the same time. The calabar tree resolves the dispute. If you eat your bean and die, then you were in the wrong. If you eat your bean and live, then you were in the right."

"And Beogo agreed to this?"

"He was too proud to refuse," said Yakuuba. "Refusing a calabar duel is the same as admitting that you are wrong. So we met in the desert by the Naasumba calabar tree. No guns, no radios, just him and me and the calabar beans."

"What happened?"

"Beogo lost," said Yakuuba. "He would have died, but I could not let that happen. I put him on the back of my horse, took him to the nearest hospital, and waited by his bedside while doctors pumped his stomach. After that he went straight back to Ouagadougou and was off work for a month."

"You saved his life," said Kas.

"And he will never forgive me for it," said Yakuuba. "Like I told you, François Beogo is a very proud man. As long as I remain alive, he can never forget the humiliation of the calabar duel."

Jake cast his mind back to the night of the gold banquet and to their conversation with the affable, larger-than-life police commissioner. From the way he had talked that night, it was clear that Commissioner Beogo hated outlaws, but Jake had not appreciated just how bitter and personal that hatred was, nor the lengths to which he might go to get revenge on his archenemy.

There followed a long silence, and then Kas voiced the question that Jake had been afraid even to contemplate. "So what do you think, Yakuuba?" she asked. "Did Beogo have something to do with our kidnapping?"

Yakuuba bit off another piece of cola nut and chewed it with a slow sideways movement of his jaw, like a ruminating cow. "I can think of only four people in this country who would dare to mastermind an operation like that. François Beogo is one of those people."

"But you can't prove that it was him?"

The Chameleon smiled. "In Africa, princess, you can't prove anything."

Jake leaned back against a sack of millet again and stretched his limbs. He liked this young outlaw who had dedicated his life to the service of the poor. And for the first time since they had met, Jake trusted him as well.

TWENTY-SIX

By eleven o'clock in the morning the sun was high in the sky, and the stowaways on top of the Ouagadougou bus were feeling the heat. Paaté found a mat among the rooftop luggage and stretched it across the top of their den like a parasol.

Jake gazed out across the wide savannah and saw a slow-moving cloud of dust far out on the plain. "What's that?" he asked.

"Last week's cattle drive," said Paaté. "It should arrive in Ouagadougou tomorrow."

Yakuuba was frowning. "Why is it going so far south?" he said.

"It just is."

"I am not talking about the cattle drive," said Yakuuba. "I am talking about that rhinoceros beetle over there."

Jake rubbed his eyes and looked in the direction where Yakuuba was pointing. He saw a reddish insect flying alongside the bus, a meter or two from the edge of the roof rack.

"She must be miles from her host tree by now," said Yakuuba. "Why is she flying so far south?"

"Our leader does not have enough to worry him," said Paaté. "Caring for a hundred thousand poor people is not sufficient burden for his heart. He needs to worry about the country's insect life as well."

"And why is she flying in the middle of the day?" asked Yakuuba. "Rhinoceros beetles do most of their flying at night and in the early morning."

"I don't know about that," said Paaté, "but I'll tell you what the beetle's thinking. She's thinking, *Why are those people traveling on top of the bus? People usually travel inside buses. Very strange behavior.*"

They were entering Kongoussi, the town that Jake had seen from his horse the day before. On a small traffic island in the center of town a Statue of Liberty lookalike gazed up at them as they passed. On the left was a large covered market with an open-air forecourt for vegetable sellers. On the right was a hospital, a bar, and a Total gas station.

"That's odd," said Yakuuba. "It has something attached to its head."

Paaté threw up his hands in exasperation. "Enough!" he cried. "I'll catch it for you, *inshallah*, and you can examine it close up, on condition that you promise not to say another word about it." He whipped off his beret, pulled a herder's staff out of a nearby travel bag, and took a needle and thread from his top pocket.

"What are you doing?" asked Jake.

"Making a beetle catcher." Paaté wound the thread six times around the head of the staff and sewed his beret onto it. "There, perfect."

Paaté held on to the outer rail of the roof rack and leaned over toward the rhinoceros beetle. He made soft clucking noises with his tongue and positioned the beret ready to swoop. If he had seen the tree coming up on his left, he could have avoided it. As it was, an overhanging branch struck him on the shoulder and swept him clean off his perch. He hit the road with a sickening thud, and his right arm snapped like a twig.

Yakuuba was the first to react. He climbed down onto the window frame, jumped clear of the bus, rolled on the ground below, got up, and ran to the aid of his friend.

"We have to stay with them," said Jake. "Come on—there's a ladder at the back of the bus."

They picked their way over the luggage and clambered off the roof and onto the ladder. Jake climbed down until he was a couple feet off the ground, and then, air running like a cartoon character, he jumped.

He sprawled in the dust, and a second or two later so did Kas. They were shaken but unhurt. The bus drove on, oblivious, toward the Kongoussi bus stop.

Jake looked back up the road. He watched Yakuuba help Paaté to his feet and lead him gently in the direction of the hospital.

Twenty-seven

Kongoussi Hospital would have won no awards for architecture. It was a rectangular concrete block with a corrugated tin roof. Inside, it was as hot as a baker's oven. A corridor ran the length of the building, with wards on either side.

There was a long line in the waiting room, but one of the doctors noticed Paaté's spectacular broken bone and took him through to a ward straightaway. Yakuuba, Jake, and Kas followed them in.

The doctor was a gangly young man with a good-natured face and big round glasses. "My name is Dr. Saudogo," he said. "I'm going to give you a little shot of anesthetic to numb your arm."

The other bed in Paaté's ward was occupied by a teenager in the grip of a raging fever. His forehead was damp with sweat and he shivered uncontrollably. A bag of intravenous fluid hung from a stand above his head, connected to the boy's wrist via a long tube. "Visitors at last!" shouted the boy. "If ashes must be eaten, it is best for them to be eaten by a crowd."

"Abdul has cerebral malaria," whispered the doctor. "The delirium comes and goes, but don't worry, he is perfectly harmless."

"I know you!" cried Abdul, extending a trembling finger toward Yakuuba. "You busted my yellow-necked milk cow out of Burizanga cow prison last year."

Jake could not believe his ears. "Don't tell me there are prisons for cows as well as bicycles."

"Yes," said Paaté. "If a policeman finds a cow wandering on public land, he impounds it in the cow prison behind the mayor's office. The owner of the cow has to pay the mayor ten thousand francs for its release."

"Twenty-four cows he freed that night!" cried Abdul. "It was epic! The minstrels of Burizanga wrote a song to celebrate the occasion."

He began to beat time on the headboard of his bed. Yakuuba started to protest, but to no avail; Abdul was determined to sing the Burizanga cow liberation song.

"He saw the guards and he saw the lock and he saw
the hoof-proof door, OH

He saw the guards and he saw the lock and he pitied

    the plight of the poor, SO

He tricked the guards and he picked the lock and

    released the twenty-four, MOO!

He tricked the guards and he picked the lock and his

    name's YAKUUBA SOR!"

The doctor looked up sharply from his work when he heard Sor's name.

"Delirium," said Yakuuba. "Completely out of his mind, poor lad."

"Perhaps," said the doctor. "Or maybe that was one of his lucid moments. Either way, I am a great admirer of this Yakuuba Sor. I have heard impressive things."

Jake turned to his sister. "Stay here," he whispered. "I need the toilet."

On his way out of the hospital Jake asked one of the nurses where he might find *le WC,* and she pointed to an open-air cubicle in the far corner of the compound. It was a simple pit toilet—a hole in the ground. The mud walls and the concrete floor were covered with cockroaches, which scuttled this way and that when Jake entered.

As he stood there, another insect scuttled in. It was not a

cockroach. It was a brown beetle with a shiny head and long black horns, just like the one that had caused Paaté's accident. And Yakuuba was right: the insect was wearing several tiny attachments. There seemed to be metal antennae on its thorax and something on its head that looked very like a— *Surely not!*

"Hello, Jake," called an English voice just outside. "I would like a word with you."

Jake left the cubicle. There before him stood a white man with a ponytail. He wore a linen jacket and khaki trousers, and he was sending a text message on his phone.

"There you are," said the man, putting the phone away. "I recognize you from the photos your father showed me."

"Who are you?"

"Roy Dexter, MI6. I've come for you and your sister."

Jake bit his lip. *At last. Rescue!*

Dexter popped into the toilet cubicle holding a small tin and came out again almost straightaway.

"What is it?" asked Jake. "Is it some sort of droid? Is that a camera on its head? Is that what you used to find us?"

"Never you mind," said Dexter. "Where is your sister?"

"She's in the hospital."

"Is she hurt?"

"She's fine," said Jake. "Yakuuba was taking us home."

The agent started. *"Yakuuba Sor?"*

"Keep your hair on," said Jake. "Sor's not as bad as the police seem to think. He's been helping us."

"Helping you?"

"Taking us back to Ouaga. He wants to talk to Dad, straighten things out."

"Sure he does." Dexter drew a pistol from his jacket pocket. "Where is Sor now, Jake? Is he in the hospital?"

"You're not listening to me. Our kidnapping had nothing to do with Yakuuba. He's a good man."

"Just tell me where he is."

"Why is your hand shaking? You don't need to be afraid of Yakuuba Sor."

"Stop messing me about!" Dexter grabbed Jake by the ear. "He's in the hospital, isn't he? He's with your sister."

"Get off—you're hurting me!"

Dexter twisted Jake's ear and marched him into the hospital. A nurse shrieked when she saw the pistol and dropped the tray she was carrying. Terrified men and women shrank back against the walls of the waiting room.

"Spit it out, lad. Which ward are they in?"

"I can't remember."

"I should have let you stay kidnapped." Dexter strode up the corridor, flinging open the doors one by one. Jake stumbled alongside him, left ear first.

Ward 1. "Kirsty!" called the agent.

No reply, just pallid stares from the ward's occupants.

Ward 2. "Kirsty!"

No reply.

Ward 3. "Kirsty!"

"Yes?" said Kas, looking up. "Who are y—?" She saw the pistol and stopped dead.

"Nobody move!" cried Dexter. He marched Jake into the ward and slammed the door with his heel. Paaté, Yakuuba, Dr. Saudogo, and poor delirious Abdul found themselves staring down the barrel of a Herstal 9mm Browning.

"What's happening?" asked Kas. "Who is this?"

"He's from MI6," said Jake, "which basically means that he's a British spy."

"That's good," said the doctor. "The British are an honorable race."

"Shut up," said Dexter. "Come over here, Kirsty, and stand next to your brother."

Kas did as she was told.

"Nice disguise, princess," muttered Dexter. "Tell me, which of these four gentlemen is Yakuuba Sor?"

"Don't tell him!" cried Jake.

"*S'il vous plaît, monsieur,*" said the doctor, holding up his hands. "Can you not see that there are sick people here?"

As quick as a scorpion, Dexter raised his pistol and fired at the drip bag above Abdul's head. The bag exploded, showering the teenager with intravenous fluid. Abdul whooped and shivered and wiped his eyes.

"*Monsieur,* that liquid was quinine solution," said the doctor. "If I do not replace the bag, my patient will die."

"If you continue to fool around, you will all die," said the Englishman. "It's you, isn't it?" he added, leveling the pistol at the doctor's chest and speaking loudly, almost disguising the fear in his voice. "Yakuuba Sor, master of disguise! It takes more than a white coat to fool a secret agent."

"I doubt that," muttered Dr. Saudogo.

Yakuuba Sor raised a hand and stepped forward. "If a blind man's salt falls among stones," he said, "he will lick everything he picks up. I am your salt, *monsieur.* What is your business with me?"

"My business, Mr. Sor?" Dexter turned to him, and the pistol in his hand began to shake violently. "I have brought you a gift from Ambassador Knight and High Commissioner Beogo."

"No!" Paaté spoke from his bed, his voice thick with pain. "He wants to protect me, but I can't let him. You see, *monsieur*, *I* am Yakuuba Sor."

Dexter wheeled around and glared at Paaté.

"As it happens," said Dr. Saudogo, "you were right the first time. I am Yakuuba Sor."

"Liar," croaked Abdul, glaring at the doctor. "*I'm* Yakuuba Sor."

"Silence!" shouted the spy. "I see that I have stumbled into a nest of terrorist sympathizers. Roll up your left sleeves, all of you. I want to see which one of you has the spiderweb tattoo."

Abdul reached for his sleeve, and his hand lighted on the intravenous needle in his wrist. "Yakuuba Sor is immortal," he murmured. "Malaria or no malaria, quinine or no quinine, Yakuuba Sor will never die. You want a tattoo? I'll give you one myself!" With that he slid the needle out of his wrist, unclipped it carefully from its drip, and hurled the needle at the Englishman.

The agent fired twice and the teenager's head snapped back against the headboard. He was dead before his needle hit the ground.

He shot him. The hairs on the back of Jake's neck stood on end. *He actually shot him.*

"One down," said Dexter.

Dr. Saudogo bellowed and ran at the spy, but he was not quick enough. The spy shot him in the stomach at point-blank range, and the doctor crumpled at his feet.

"Two down," said Dexter.

"Stop!" shouted Sor. His sleeve was rolled up, exposing the spiderweb tattoo. "I'm the one you want!"

"Wait your turn," said Dexter, taking aim at Paaté.

"Jake, do something!" screamed Kas. "Your sword!"

Jake reached for the Tuareg sword in his belt, but it was no longer there. He had left it on the roof of the bus.

Paaté swung his legs off the bed and tried to stand up, cradling his broken arm in front of him. He did not stand a chance, poor lad. A shot rang out, a faraway look came into Paaté's eyes, and he gazed down at the hole in his chest. Then he coughed and slumped over sideways onto the bed. Kas howled like a wounded animal and buried her face in her hands.

"Three down," said Dexter, swiveling to point the pistol at Sor. He glanced at the spiderweb tattoo and shook his head. "You have very loyal friends, Mr. Sor, and now you will be joining them."

The outlaw must have known he was about to die, but he did not seem to care much. He took Paaté's hand in his own and stroked it. *"Désolé, Paaté,"* he whispered. *I'm so very sorry.*

Dexter squeezed the trigger and a fourth bang resounded through the ward. The bullet ricocheted off the concrete wall behind Yakuuba and shattered a window. The outlaw was unscathed.

"You missed." Sor's voice was devoid of emotion. "Try again."

Dexter frowned and leveled the pistol at the outlaw's head.

"My name is Yakuuba," said Sor. "Yakuuba Sor, Friend of the Poor. Damn your red ears!"

Dexter blinked and seemed to sway a little.

Then Jake saw it. Sticking into the gunman's ankle, not far from the dying doctor's outstretched hand, was an empty anesthetic syringe.

Dexter's eyelids flickered. He scowled at his trigger finger, willing it to obey him. Then he staggered backward three or four paces and crumpled to the ground. His pistol clattered on the polished cement floor.

After that, the ward was full of people, all talking and shouting at once.

Twenty-eight

Jake hugged his knees and pressed himself against the wall. He had never seen anyone die before today, let alone be shot, and now he had seen three people murdered in the space of half a minute. It was too much to take in.

Kas was crying. "We didn't do a thing," she said. "We just watched it happen."

"We had no choice." Jake's voice sounded hollow in his own ears.

"We just sat and watched them die like it was a video game."

"There was nothing we could have done."

Some of the people in the ward were doctors and nurses, others were patients or relatives of patients. Some wept, others shouted, others stood still and stared. Attempts were made to resuscitate Dr. Saudogo, but in vain.

Yakuuba appeared in front of them. He was blinking a lot and seemed to be having trouble focusing. "Let's go," he said.

"Go?" Jake stared at him. "But what about Paaté?"

"Paaté is dead. I have closed his eyelids."

"But surely you want to stay and—"

"They are dead, all three of them, and the people of Kongoussi will give them honorable burials. But right now we must do what Paaté would have wanted us to do."

"Which is?"

"To leave," said Yakuuba. "The police will be here in thirty seconds."

Jake looked out the shattered window. Armed police were swarming into the compound and sprinting in the direction of the hospital.

"Follow me," said Yakuuba. "When I move, you move."

They hurried out of the ward into a crowd of people moving this way and that. The *gendarmes* had blocked off the doors at both ends of the building and were advancing along the corridor in a pincer movement.

Yakuuba dived left into an empty examining room, followed by Jake and Kas.

The outlaw slipped off his STMB overalls and baseball cap

and donned a white coat. "You see what I mean?" he said, poking Jake hard in the chest. "Strike first, ask questions later! You people are all the same."

"That man was terrified of you," said Jake. "He was completely out of control."

"What about your father? Is your father also terrified of me? Is your father going to shoot us all on sight?"

"No," said Jake. "Dad knows how to ask questions, even when he is frightened." He hoped it was true.

Yakuuba opened a window and climbed out into the bushes. Jake and Kas followed.

"Try to keep cool heads," said Yakuuba. "We are going to walk across the compound in full view of the police. Walk, not run, do you understand? Go!"

Jake's legs felt so shaky that simply walking in a straight line took all his concentration. They set off, heading for the motorcycle parking spaces along the east wall. Two *gendarmes* ran past them in the opposite direction, guns in hand.

Reaching the motorcycle parking lot, Yakuuba walked quickly between the rows, turning his head from side to side to examine the bikes.

"What are you looking for?" asked Jake.

"We're looking for a Kaiser 150cc scooter. It's Dr. Saudogo's bike."

"How do you know what bike he has?"

Sor held up a small key. "I make it my business to recognize bike keys."

"Where did you get that?"

"I took it from the doctor's body."

"You're not serious."

"The doctor gave his life for me, Jake. Do you think he would begrudge me his moped?"

Sor found the bike he was looking for—a gleaming black scooter with chrome handlebars and a luggage rack.

"Look," said Kas. "They've got two men on the gate. They've blocked our only way out."

"One of us will have to draw them away," said Yakuuba.

"I'll do it," Jake heard himself say. "When they see me walk up the wall, they'll come after me."

Yakuuba looked at him. "Walk up the wall?"

Jake nodded. "Watch." He walked toward the gate and then, when he was sure that the guards had noticed him, he veered right and broke into a run.

"*Arrêtes-toi!*" cried the *gendarmes* at the gate. "Stop!"

Behind him, Jake heard the click and growl of the Kaiser starting up.

The wall of the hospital compound was about ten feet high, and the parapet was smooth. Under normal circumstances it would be an easy hop. Jake accelerated toward the wall with short quick strides, took off from his right foot, placed his left foot at chest height, and was about to launch himself upward when a shot rang out. It was only a warning shot, but it was more than enough to shake his concentration. His left foot slipped, and he crashed into the wall and crumpled to the ground.

The *gendarmes* had abandoned their post at the gate and were running toward him, their arms already stretched out for the anticipated arrest. Beyond the *gendarmes* Jake saw Yakuuba and Kas on the moped, heading for the exit at full tilt.

Shaken but unhurt, he got quickly to his feet, took three quick steps back, then powered forward and up the wall. This time his eyes were fixed on the goal, and his feet were quick and sure. He scrabbled with his hands and the balls of his feet and—*reach!*—he grabbed the parapet.

One of the *gendarmes* made a lunge for his feet, but Jake curled up his legs in the nick of time. He flexed his wrists, bent his arms, and clambered up and over.

"Arrêtes-toi!" repeated the *gendarmes,* but Jake had no intention of stopping now. He dropped down on the far side of the wall and looked around him. He was in some sort of outdoor café bar, and this being the hottest time of day, it was doing good business. A dozen plump, sharp-suited businessmen were sitting at a long trestle table cradling their bottles of beer and staring straight at him.

"Bonjour," muttered Jake. He ran past them, jumped up onto the drinks bar in front of an astonished barman, vaulted another wall, and landed in the forecourt of the Total gas station.

"Tuubaaku, we're here!" Yakuuba pulled up on the moped, waited a fraction of a second for Jake to clamber on, and then set off again. He swerved out into the traffic, beeping the horn and twisting the throttle so hard that the engine screamed.

The Kaiser 150 was a decent enough bike, but it was not built for three. Perched all the way at the back on the flimsy chrome luggage rack, Jake had to contort his legs to keep his feet from dragging along the ground. What was more, there were two police bikes behind them. The police bikes were bigger and more powerful than the Kaiser, and they pursued their prey with the confidence and menace of black panthers.

"Hold on tight," said the outlaw, squeezing the back brake gently and stamping on the front brake. The back wheel shot out and Yakuuba pulled the handlebars to one side. Kas screamed. Jake's knee grazed the macadam as they completed the U-turn.

"Don't tense up in the turns, or you'll flip the bike," said the outlaw. "Just let your bodies go floppy."

Going floppy was easier said than done. Yakuuba leaned hard right and plunged down a concrete bank into the pedestrians-only vegetable market. Eggplants flew. Onions rolled. Traders yelped and swore. A cloud of millet flour rose from a ruptured sack like smoke.

Jake looked back and saw that their pursuers were still behind them, but the superior speed and power of the police bikes was neutralized off-road. Here in the vegetable market it was maneuverability—nippiness—that was needed, and the Kaiser had it in spades.

On they rode into the dark narrow aisles of the covered market. Beads, bangles, mosquito coils, cement bags, water pistols, hair extensions, electric fans, red and yellow energy pills, stilettos, firecrackers, reggae CDs, sprockets—a whole Aladdin's cave of knickknacks swept past them in a blur, while terrified vendors dived out of the way.

"Ko jawo weli fuu, wo daabawal buri welde!" shouted Yakuuba. "The bangle is sweet, but the wrist is sweeter!"

There had always been a devil-may-care attitude about the outlaw, but the way he was riding now was suicidal. He gripped the throttle and gunned it to the max, perhaps hoping that savage breakneck speed would blast away his grief. White-knuckled, they tore out of the covered market and shot blinking into the light. Straight across a busy road, up into the cloisters of a mosque, past a line of blind men begging for change, down a flight of steps, across a soccer field, and into a forest.

The forest floor was studded with vicious acacia thorns, which ripped the tires to shreds. When they finally limped out of the forest, they were riding on the Kaiser's wheel rims.

There in front of them was a massive lake. A large herd of cows stood drinking in the shallows, while the herders washed and waded. The men had discarded their cloaks and their conical herder hats on a rock at the water's edge.

"Just as I hoped!" exclaimed Yakuuba. "It's the cattle drive we saw earlier. Get off the bike, *tuubaakus*, and find a cow to hide behind."

Jake and Kas got off the bike. Yakuuba revved the accelerator, released the clutch, and shot off toward the lake, weaving his way among the startled cows. On reaching the lake, he leaped off onto the mud flats. The Kaiser plowed on into the murky water, where it gurgled, spluttered, and sank.

The herders gaped, and the oldest of them let forth a torrent of French expletives.

"Si a yi'ii bojjel na dogga fuu, ndara gada," said Yakuuba, picking up a cloak and a herder hat from the rock. "If you see a rabbit running, look behind it."

"Who is chasing you?"

Yakuuba slipped the cloak over the doctor's coat and put the hat on his head. "Police," he said. "I am Yakuuba Sor."

The old herder blinked and narrowed his eyes. Then his face cracked into a grin of recognition. "Indeed you are!" he cried. "I did not recognize you."

"I am traveling with two friends." Sor pointed at Jake and Kas. "We need refuge."

"Granted," said the old man. He grabbed the nearest cow and led it out of the water and up the bank, obliterating the Kaiser's tire tracks.

Jake and Kas each hid behind a large cow, lining up their feet with the cows' hooves as best they could. They were just in time. A moment later two police bikes burst out of the forest and skidded to a halt on the bank. Jake did not dare lift his head to look, but he heard every word.

"*Salut*, old man," said one of the *gendarmes*. "We are looking for three fugitives on a motorbike."

"What kind of motorbike?"

"A Kaiser 150."

"Yes, I believe I did see a bike like that."

"When? Where?"

"Three days ago in Burizanga. I brushed my teeth in its wing mirror."

"I'm talking about today," said the *gendarme*. "Right here, less than a minute ago."

"Today?" The old man hemmed and hawed. "No, *monsieur*. I do not believe that such a bike has come our way today. But let me ask my son. Hamadu, have you seen a Kaiser 150 in these parts today?"

"I don't believe I have, Father," said Yakuuba Sor. "Not today."

TWENTY-NINE

When the police were gone, Yakuuba Sor approached the man and shook his hand. *"Yitere woyatanaa mo anndi,"* he said. "The eye cries over him who is known."

"Who?" asked the old man.

"Paaté Tamboura," said Sor, looking out over the lake.

"I am sorry to hear it. May God forgive his sins and reward his charity."

"Amen," said Yakuuba.

"May he inherit blessing."

"Amen."

"May he drink the water of paradise."

"Amen."

"I was friends with his father. My name is Idrissa."

"I know."

Idrissa touched his forehead—a gesture of respect for the dead. Then he turned to look at Jake and Kas. "Tuaregs?"

"*Tuubaakus*," said the outlaw. "I am taking them to Ouagadougou."

"Then you must walk with us. Our cattle trails are far from the main road and far from the police. We shall walk together and arrive in Ouagadougou unmolested, *inshallah*."

"Thank you," said Yakuuba, and the cattle drive moved off.

A tall thin man called Macha walked at the front, chirruping loudly to announce the way. The cows followed, ninety-six of them in total, their long, curved horns shining in the midday sun. They were flanked by two young men, Boureima and Diallo, and whenever a cow strayed too far to one side, one of them would run to head it off, twirling a staff to coax the errant cow back into the herd. Usually a word or a gesture was enough to motivate a cow, but occasionally the sharp *thwack* of wood on hide would ring out across the plains.

Jake and Kas brought up the rear with Idrissa. The wrinkles on the old man's face told a story of great suffering and regular laughter. He swung his staff, held his chin high, and walked with a spring in his step. Not so the cows. Exhausted by a week of travel, they dragged their hooves along the ground and disturbed great clouds of reddish dust, which floated away to the west.

Yakuuba walked in the middle of the dust cloud, holding his hat over his nose and mouth. Once or twice Boureima tried to talk to him, but the outlaw was not in the mood for conversation.

"It is very hard for him," Idrissa said to Jake. "He knew Paaté all his life. They grew up together on the Baraboulé plains, riding donkeys and shooting lizards with their slingshots. When they were seven years old, they went to Mali and studied together under Amadou Hampaté Ba. When they were twelve, they founded the Friends of the Poor together. They have always been like brothers."

Jake clenched his teeth and looked away, replaying the hospital massacre in his mind for the hundredth time. How on earth could it have happened? What was his father playing at, sending a complete nut job to their rescue?

"Is this the first time you have ever followed a cattle drive?" asked Idrissa.

"Yes," said Jake.

"It is the hardest job on earth," said Idrissa. "After three days, your head starts aching. After five days, your legs start aching. After seven days, your lower back starts aching. And the thirst! I cannot begin to describe the thirst. Do not look so worried, *tuubaaku*. You only have one day of walking. Tomorrow lunchtime, *inshallah*, we arrive in Ouagadougou, and our patron will pay us ten thousand francs each."

Jake drew a fold of his turban up over his mouth and nose. *Ten thousand francs*, he thought. *Twelve pounds fifty in English money. For eight days and nights of grueling work.*

One foot in front of the other, on they walked, hammered relentlessly by the African sun. Jake's mouth was parched and his eyes ached from the intense light. He could feel Kas close beside him, but for an hour and a half they did not exchange a single word.

At three o'clock they came across a water pump in the middle of nowhere. A beaming African woman interrupted her pumping to let the herders drink directly from the standpipe. Clear, cool water gushed against their palates, ran down their chins, and drenched their robes.

"Allahu akbar!" cried Idrissa, drying his face with his sleeve. "I have come back from the dead!"

At that moment Jake heard the choppy whir of rotor blades. A helicopter came into sight, flying low above the treetops and heading their way.

"Hats!" yelled Yakuuba, the first word he had spoken all afternoon.

Boureima threw his herder hat to Jake. Diallo threw his to Kas. The helicopter passed overhead and yammered off toward Kongoussi.

When night fell, the herders pitched their camp next to a dry well half a mile south of a village called Sogolzi. While the cows grazed, Idrissa, Diallo, and Boureima performed their twilight prayers—standing, bowing, and kneeling toward the east. Macha went into the village and came back with a bowl of *sagabo,* an enormous whitish dumpling made of maize.

Idrissa nodded ruefully. "You know you are close to Ouagadougou when the only food you can buy is *sagabo.* Thank heaven I have sugar in my satchel."

"I will watch the cows while the rest of you eat," said Yakuuba. He sat down beside the dry well and rested his chin on his hands.

Boureima milked two of the cows, and then the meal began. Crouching around a single bowl, they took turns breaking off handfuls of the still-warm dumpling.

When the bowl was empty, Idrissa reclined on his elbows and sighed. *"Ah hamdilillalay!"* he exclaimed. "God did not give us *nyiiri* tonight, but we have eaten our fill of *sagabo* and we shall still be alive in the morning, *inshallah.*"

The cows were full as well. They stopped grazing, and some of them lay down. Others stood and stared, their crescent horns and parabolic humps silhouetted in the moonlight.

"Where do we sleep?" asked Kas.

"Right here, on God's own mattress," said Idrissa, patting the ground affectionately.

Kas blanched. "What about the snakes?"

"They will sleep on the ground as well."

"No, what I meant was—"

"I know what you meant," said Idrissa, his shoulders shaking with laughter. "Do not worry, *tuubaaku*. I have slept on the ground in the open air too many times to count, and in my whole life I have had only two snake bites."

"*Two?*" Kas did not sound reassured, but she lay down anyway and closed her eyes.

Jake went and sat down next to Yakuuba. "You must be hungry," he said.

Yakuuba shook his head and threw a small stone into the dry well.

"I'm sorry," said Jake. "I should have reacted quicker. I could have grabbed the gun before he started shooting. I was the closest to him. If I had grabbed the gun, you could have come and helped me, and Paaté would be—"

"Paaté would still be dead," said Yakuuba. "Such things are written." He reached into his trouser pocket and took out Jake's phone. "I have never seen a phone like this," he said matter-of-factly.

"It is a clever phone," said Jake, unsure of the French for smartphone.

"It takes pictures?"

"And video."

"Show me."

Jake took the phone and opened up the folder "Africa Vids." The first clip in the folder was the panorama he had captured on arriving at the gold banquet: golden chandeliers and candlesticks, crisp white table linen, shining vases full of fire orchids, and crowds of idle rich.

"Who are all these people?" asked Yakuuba.

"Gold barons. You once haunted their mine."

"*Allahu akbar*," Yakuuba murmured. "*Hoore waawnde roondaade lefol buge na waawi roondaade ledde*. A head that wears a crown can also carry firewood."

"What does that mean?"

"Two nights ago you feasted in a banqueting hall made of gold, and tonight you ate *sagabo* with your fingers, sitting on the bare ground—" Sor broke off suddenly and craned his neck to stare at the screen up close.

"What's wrong?"

"Play that clip again," said Yakuuba. "Look in the farthest corner of the hall, on the left there in the shadows."

Jake paused the video and pinched the LCD screen to zoom in. "Two men talking," he said. "So what?"

"The one on the left is Commissioner Beogo," said Yakuuba. "And with him, if I am not mistaken, is the man who chased me in Djibo this morning."

Jake looked again. In spite of the low resolution, Beogo was indeed recognizable. As for the other man—Jake zoomed in some more—yes, Yakuuba was right about him, too. It was the *gendarme*, their kidnapper, wearing his waiter disguise.

Jake's head swam. All this time he had been carrying in his pocket the evidence they needed: proof of a link between their kidnapper and Police Commissioner Beogo himself.

"Well spotted, Yakuuba!" he cried. "Just wait until Dad sees this! Beogo is going to have a lot of explaining to do."

"*Faa faa rimataake,*" replied Sor. "Until until is never born! Stay on your guard, my friend—we are not in Ouagadougou yet."

Thirty

Jake did not sleep well. Sor's warning to stay on their guard did not help; nor did God's own mattress. When Jake lay on his back, his shoulder blades and tailbone hurt. When he lay on his side, his ribs and pelvis hurt. But most unsettling of all were the terrible memories of the day just gone. Whenever he closed his eyes and began to dream, he saw an action replay of the Kongoussi massacre and woke up with a start. In the end he stopped trying to sleep altogether. He preferred to gaze at the stars all night rather than be forced to revisit that terrible ward one more time.

Kas was having a hard time too. She was curled up in the fetal position with her head in the crook of her arm, but her eyes were wide open.

"Hello," whispered Jake. "Can't you sleep either?"

"No. I keep thinking about—"

"Me too."

"What time is it?"

"Midnight."

Jake sat up and looked around. All the herders were wide-awake. Boureima sat to the north of the cows, Diallo to the east, Macha to the south, and Idrissa to the west.

Suddenly Jake heard the sound of running footsteps right behind him. He jumped up and turned around, blood pounding in his ears.

Yakuuba Sor burst out of the black night, ran around to the south side of the herd, and grabbed Macha by the scruff of the neck. "It was you, wasn't it?" he snarled in French, shaking the lanky herder until his teeth rattled.

"I don't know what you mean!"

"When you went into Sogolzi to buy *sagabo,* you told the villagers about the *tuubaaku* children."

"I never!" Macha shook his head.

Old Idrissa hurried toward them. "Tell him the truth, Macha," he said. "Deceit cannot trick the son of a djinn."

Macha scowled and tried to break away, but to no avail. "All right," he said. "I told the villagers. And they told me about the two-hundred-thousand-franc reward being offered by their father for the return of his children. That money is the reason the Chameleon is so intent on seeing his *tuubaakus* safely home. And that is why he chose us to aid him in his getaway. We are the only four people in the country who have not listened to a radio in the last week. *The only people who would not demand a share of his winnings.*"

Idrissa clapped his wrinkled hand over Macha's mouth. "Enough of your babbling," he cried. "The Friends of the Poor are only one step lower than the angels of heaven themselves. If you ever again insult the Chameleon in my presence, I will take my staff to you."

Macha scowled, and fierce tears welled in his eyes.

Yakuuba let go of the herder's scrawny neck. "I forgive you, Macha," he said. "After seven sunny days and seven wakeful nights even the strongest head may addle. As for the reward—"

"No!" cried Idrissa. "We do not want to hear it. You have always done what is right, Yakuuba, and you have our absolute trust. The important thing now is that we plan our next step wisely. What are the men of Sogolzi doing?"

"The elders are talking in the Palaver Hut," said Yakuuba. "They are planning to capture the *tuubaakus* by force and claim the reward for themselves. The young men of the village will attack us within the hour."

"We shall fight them off!" cried Diallo, unsheathing his machete.

"We would not stand a chance. The village of Sogolzi has thirty fighting men."

"Then we must run away!"

"Impossible," said Yakuuba. "They have two horses and eight motorcycles. They would catch us easily." He closed his eyes and thought for a very long time. "Idrissa," he said at last. "How much sugar do you have left?"

"A one-pound bag."

"That will suffice," the outlaw said, then turned to Jake and looked him up and down. "I am sorry, *tuubaaku.*"

"Why are you sorry?" asked Jake, the hairs rising on the back of his neck.

"I am sorry for what I am about to ask of you. Tonight you are going to make a very great sacrifice."

Thirty-one

Salif Yako, eldest son of the village chief, donned his leather hunting boots, slung a quiver of arrows over his shoulder, picked up his bow, and hurried outside to join his men in front of the village mosque. He stepped up before them and shone his flashlight over the ranks. The Sogolzi fighting core was a spirited rabble composed of farmers, hunters, and blacksmiths. They were passionate and loyal and long overdue for a scrap.

The men were armed each according to his trade: The farmers wielded hoes and machetes, the hunters carried bows and slingshots, the blacksmiths had brought clubs and hammers. Some of the men carried kerosene lamps, others held flashlights, and their ranks pulsed with fiery optimism. Tonight the numbers were clearly on their side—thirty experienced fighting men versus five cattle drivers and two children. If they got the pitched battle they longed for, it would very soon be over.

Salif led his men out of the village and across the plain toward the herders' camp, a distance of about half a mile. But when they arrived, the camp was empty. A wisp of smoke rose from the campfire. Cattle tracks led southward into the night.

"This cattle dung is fresh!" cried Bukari the hunter. "They are not long gone. If we move fast, we will overtake them within the hour."

"After them!" cried a blacksmith, waving his club high in the air.

"Don't let them get away!"

"Wait!" Something had caught Salif's attention—a square of parchment skewered on the thorns of an acacia tree. "They have left a message for us. Do any of you men know how to read Arabic?"

الـثروة الـتي تبحث غنها هي في البئر

Faruk the maize farmer stepped forward. "My grandfather was an imam," he said. "He taught me Arabic when I was just a lad." Faruk took the parchment and examined the spidery writing. "'The wealth you seek is in the well.'"

"In the well, he says!"

"The wealth we seek is in the well!"

All thirty men rushed to the dry well. They shone their flashlights down the shaft, but it was fifty meters deep, and even with their flashlights they could not see the bottom.

"Listen!" cried Salif. "I think there's somebody down there."

The men shushed each other loudly and then fell silent.

"Help!" A frightened English voice came from the well. "Somebody please help!"

"That's *tuubaaku* language!" whispered Salif. "Those fiends have thrown the *tuubaaku* boy into the well."

They listened again, and now there were two voices shouting in unison, a boy and a girl. The girl was sobbing as she shouted for help, a truly heart-wrenching sound.

"Why would the herders disappear and leave both of their *tuubaakus* down the well?" said Hassan.

"They must have known we were coming," said Faruk.

"I agree," said Salif. "They dared not fight, so instead they have given us what we wanted."

A murmur of disappointment rippled through the ranks. Those feeble cattle drivers had handed Sogolzi the victory and spoiled all the fun. The bows and hoes would not be called upon tonight. But at least the *tuubaakus* were now in their possession.

With judicious negotiation, perhaps they could persuade the father to double the reward.

"Somebody get us out of here!" The children were getting desperate now, and their faint but frantic shouts from the well brought the men back to the task at hand.

"How are we going to get the *tuubaakus* out?" asked Bogodolo the blacksmith, ever practical. "Those vagabonds have cut off the rope at the crossbar."

"So they have!"

"They've taken our rope!"

"The rope is down here!" yelled the girl in the well, and this time she spoke French. "They threw the rope in after us!"

"Did you hear that?" said Faruk, outraged. "She says they threw the rope in after them!"

Salif sat down on the edge of the well and rubbed his stubbly jaw. It made perfect sense, of course. If the herders had not cut the rope, the *tuubaakus* would have simply waited until the coast was clear, climbed up the rope, and escaped into the bush.

"We need another rope," said Salif. "Does anyone here own a fifty-meter length?"

"No."

"Not me."

"What about shorter lengths?" asked Salif. "My father uses two five-meter ropes to tie up his horses."

"I have a two-meter length of rope at home," said Faruk. "I use it to tether my goat."

"Me too!" cried several voices.

"Good," said Salif. "Let everyone who has rope go and fetch it. The rest of us will stay here and guard the well."

Half an hour later the men returned with their ropes, and they began the painstaking process of tying them together.

"Make sure your knots are good!" cried Salif. "If a single knot slips, the rope will break and the *tuubaakus* will plummet to their deaths."

"The rope is down here!" yelled the girl in the well. "They threw the rope in after us!"

"We heard you!" shouted Salif. "Be patient—we will have you out of there in no time!"

In twenty minutes the new rope was ready. It was not a handsome rope, but it was strong, and the knots would make good footholds for the *tuubaakus* to climb up. Bogodolo the blacksmith tied one end of the rope to the crossbar of the well and threw the other end down the shaft. Down and down it slithered until it reached the bottom.

"There's rope for you!" Salif shouted down the shaft. "Climb up nice and slow."

"Help!" came the frightened reply. "Somebody please help us!"

"Grab the rope!" yelled Salif. "We can pull you up ourselves if need be. Just grab it and hold on tight!"

"Somebody get us out of here!"

"I can't stand this," said Salif. He shrugged off his quiver and shoved a flashlight into his belt. He stepped up onto the side of the well, grabbed the makeshift rope in both hands, and let it take his weight. "I'm going in."

Hand over hand, foot over foot, down into the darkness Salif Yako climbed, praying that the knots would hold. "I'm coming down to get you, *tuubaakus*!" he called. "Don't be afraid!"

"The rope is down here!" the girl yelled back. "They threw the rope in after us!"

Five minutes later Salif's feet touched down on the sand at the bottom of the well. The white-knuckle climb was over, God be praised. He switched on his flashlight and shone it around. The old well rope lay in coils at his feet, still attached to its rusty water bucket. The two *tuubaakus* were nowhere to be seen!

"Help!" came a voice from the bucket. "Somebody help us!"

With trembling fingers Salif moved the rope aside, reached into the bucket, and felt around. His fingers closed on a small plastic box, about the size of a cigarette packet, only thinner. It was a mobile phone, and it was sobbing loudly. Emblazoned across the screen were five words in a language Salif did not understand.

Now playing: help.mp3 (loop)

Seething with anger, Salif Yako pocketed the phone, tied the two ends of rope together, and climbed back up the well shaft. By now the cattle drive was at least an hour ahead of them, probably much more. "We've been tricked!" he cried as he climbed up into the open air. "Saddle the horses! Prepare the motorcycles! We must pursue those vagabonds!"

The first person he saw when he emerged from the well was his father, Al Hajji Yako Tijani, chief of Sogolzi. The chief was leaning on his walking stick, his craggy wrinkled face lit from below by a flickering kerosene lamp. "Pursuit will be impossible," said the old man. "Both my horses have been stolen, and the saddles too. With the village empty of young men, there was nothing I could do to stop it."

"What about the motorcycles?"

"Sabotaged before my very eyes," said the chief. "Those *tuubaaku* fiends put sugar in the fuel tanks."

Thirty-Two

Two horses trotted side by side through dense savannah, heading toward a glow on the southern horizon. It was four o'clock in the morning, but Burkina Faso's capital city never sleeps. Its bonfires and neon strip lights would burn right through till sunrise.

"Ouagadougou awaits," said Yakuuba. "Princess Kadija and her brother Ali are coming home at last!"

Since leaving Sogolzi they had been riding for three hours, and before long they would be in the big city. Yakuuba rode the chief's palomino mare, while Jake and Kas rode his gray stallion.

"That whole village must be hopping mad," said Kas.

"Don't feel too sorry for them," said Yakuuba. "Sooner or later they are going to realize how much your brother's phone is worth. And if they get a fair price for it at market, they can use the proceeds to buy three horses!"

"Five, more like," Jake muttered.

A few days ago Jake would have been deeply upset about sacrificing his most precious possession. But recent events, particularly Paaté's death, had changed his outlook. *The bangle is sweet,* he said to himself, *but the wrist is far, far sweeter.*

The travelers arrived in Ouagadougou at sunrise. They dismounted on the northern edge of the city, gave the horses to an astonished beggar at the roadside, and continued their journey on foot.

All along the sidewalk young men and women were swinging open the awnings of their bookshops, hardware stores, and telephone booths. The roads were busy with bicycles, mopeds, donkey carts, and taxis—adults on their way to work and children on their way to school.

Jake, Kas, and Yakuuba passed through the capital's *grand marché,* a sprawling concrete labyrinth crammed with sandals, drums, carvings, motorcycle parts, and pickpockets. They headed past the president's palace, along Avenue Charles de Gaulle, and into the leafy groves of Embassy Row.

"*Zut*," said Jake, stopping in his tracks.

"What's wrong?"

"I can see the gates of the British embassy, and there's a guard."

"There's always a guard," said Kas. "His name is Saalu, remember?"

"I don't mean Saalu," said Jake. "I mean a whole flipping platoon of *gendarmes*."

"I expected something like this," whispered Yakuuba. "Beogo must have guessed that I would bring you here. His last hope is to militarize the embassy compound."

"Let's find a telephone and call Mum and Dad," suggested Kas.

Yakuuba shook his head. "Whatever you say to your parents over the phone, you can guarantee that Beogo will be listening in. One of you needs to get in there and talk to your parents in person. Make them understand what is really going on here. And make them get rid of the *gendarmes*."

Brother and sister looked at each other. "I'll do it," said Jake. "By law that compound is a little slice of Britain. Once I'm inside the gate, they can't touch me."

"You can't do your wall stunt thingy here," said Kas. "The walls of the embassy are topped with broken glass, remember?"

Thirty-Three

Jake approached the embassy from the back, and as he passed the Zone du Bois mosque, he saw a small prayer mat on the step outside. *That'll do.* He grabbed the mat and put it under his arm, bracing himself to run if challenged.

There in front of him loomed the back wall of the embassy, twelve feet high and topped with glass. He sprinted toward it with short quick strides, kicked off the wall at chest height, and launched himself upward. As he did so, he threw the mat onto the parapet, where it snagged on the broken glass. Another small kick from his right foot, and—*reach!*—he grabbed the top of the wall through the thick mat. Hard fragments of glass cut deep into the coarse fabric, and one vicious shard gashed his palm. The sudden pain made his head spin.

He hoisted himself over the parapet and scrambled down the inside of the wall, landing as softly as he could. He darted behind the shed, where he was able to watch the movements of the guards. In addition to those at the gate, there were two *gendarmes* patrolling inside the perimeter wall—one clockwise, the other counterclockwise. Jake waited behind the shed until the guards passed each other, then scurried quietly through the gap between them. He reached the house, swung himself up onto the veranda, and tried the front door. It was open.

Jake stood in the hallway. "Hello?" he called.

His mum appeared at the living-room door. She put her hand to her mouth and stared at her son is disbelief, then ran to him and gathered him into a tight hug. She was crying, and Jake may have been as well for all he knew.

His father was not far behind. He looked far from his usual dapper self; his shirt was crumpled, his face was unshaven, and dark bags of skin hung under his eyes. Jake would have been willing to bet that his father's first word would be "Capital!" but he would have been wrong. Instead, the ambassador pumped the air with his fist and shrieked "YES!" with a ferocity that made his son jump.

The questions were not far behind. *Jake, are you all right? Where is Kirsty? Are you hurt? Why is your hand bleeding?*

"I'm fine. She's nearby," answered Jake to the first two questions. "She couldn't get in the gate."

"Why not?"

"Too many *gendarmes*."

"Special forces," said Mr. Knight. "They're here for our protection."

"No, they aren't. They're here to stop Kas and me from getting in and talking to you."

Someone else slid into view behind the ambassador. Jake recognized the square jaw, the wavy hair, and the piercing blue eyes. His stomach lurched, and he fought off competing impulses to run and to throw up.

"Hello, Jake," said Dexter. "I'm so glad you managed to escape."

"What is he doing here?" shouted Jake.

"Roy has been briefing us over coffee," said Mrs. Knight. "He has been working very hard to find you two."

"He's a monster," cried Jake. "He shot three innocent people."

"Roy told us about the incident at the hospital," said Mr. Knight. "He has submitted a full report to the Foreign Office, and they are satisfied that any deaths were unavoidable."

"Unavoidable!" Jake clenched his fists. "He killed a doctor, a sick man, and a harmless teenager, all in cold blood."

"It's called collateral damage," said Mr. Knight. "Dexter

has a license to kill, and occasionally he must use it. All the intelligence regarding Yakuuba Sor shows that he is a ruthless criminal running a terrorist training camp. When the Foreign Office saw that ransom video of yours, they ordered Dexter to—"

"Dad, you don't understand. Yakuuba had nothing to do with that ransom video. Our kidnappers were *gendarmes*."

"But the tattoo . . ."

"The tattoo was fake."

Mr. Knight frowned. "Jake," he said gently, "have you ever heard of Stockholm syndrome?"

"No."

"It's where a hostage falls in love with his or her kidnapper. It's not uncommon. There are psychological reasons for—"

"I'm not in love with Sor," said Jake angrily, "and he's not my kidnapper. He's the good guy in all of this, and Beogo's trying to set him up."

"Beogo! You can't be serious."

"Yakuuba wants to speak with you, Dad. We told him he could trust you."

Jake's mother put a hand to her throat. "Are you saying that Yakuuba Sor is here in Ouagadougou?"

"Yes."

"And he still has Kirsty?"

"We traveled together, if that's what you mean. When the muezzin starts his call to Friday prayers, they will come past the gate with the crowds. Yakuuba wants to know if you can guarantee him refuge."

"I suppose we'll have to," said the ambassador.

Roy Dexter's jaw dropped. "With respect, sir, we're talking about the most wanted man in the country, and you are a high-ranking diplomat. You can't be seen to harbor criminals."

The ambassador held up a thin, white hand. "Mr. Dexter," he said, "I'd harbor a spitting cobra if it brought my daughter back to me."

When the call to prayer began to sound from the minaret behind the embassy, Jake and his parents went out into the front yard, followed by Dexter. The police lieutenant guarding the gate was amazed to see Jake.

"How did he—?"

"He walks up walls," said the ambassador. "Open that gate."

The policeman opened the gate. Friday prayers were about to begin, and people started filing past the open gate, hurrying toward the mosque. Eagerly Jake scanned the faces in the crowd.

"Lieutenant Ouedraogo," said Mr. Knight, "are you aware of the Treaty of Vienna?"

"Of course."

"It's a set of international laws that govern diplomatic relations."

"I know what it is."

"Article Twenty-three states that embassy premises are inviolable and may not be entered or searched except with the consent of the ambassador. The receiving state—that's you and your men, Lieutenant—has a special duty to protect the embassy from any disturbance of its peace or impairment of its dignity."

"I know that."

"Of course you do. I only mention it because I intend to grant temporary refuge to a man called Yakuuba Sor, and I expect your full cooperation."

The lieutenant stared. "*Monsieur l'Ambassadeur,* you cannot expect us to—"

"Kirsty!" Mrs. Knight started forward, opening her arms wide. Kas ducked out of the passing crowd and flew into her mother's waiting embrace.

A young man strolled in after her. He wore a prayer hat and

a long white robe. *"Salaam aleykum,"* he said, and every police-man in the compound went for his gun.

"Aleykum asalaam, Yakuuba Sor," said the ambassador. "You are welcome here."

"Am I?" said Sor. There were four gun barrels pointing at his head.

"Lieutenant, *control your men!*" The ambassador's voice was cold as ice.

"But *monsieur,* he might be armed."

"Mr. Dexter, please ascertain whether our guest is carrying a weapon."

Yakuuba stared with loathing at the man who had killed his best friend. But he submitted to the search without saying a word.

"He's carrying, all right," said Dexter, having frisked the outlaw thoroughly.

"That's a slingshot," said Jake. "He takes it with him everywhere."

"Hardly a rocket launcher," his father agreed. "All the same, Dexter, perhaps you should hang on to it until we are finished."

"Finished with what?" asked the lieutenant.

"With our discussions," said Mr. Knight. "My family and I will go into the embassy residence now. Mr. Dexter and

Yakuuba Sor will accompany us. The rest of you will wait outside and protect the compound from any disturbance of its peace or impairment of its dignity."

"This is an outrage!" cried the lieutenant. "I am going to call Commissioner Beogo this instant."

"You do that," said Mr. Knight. He turned on his heel and led the way up the steps and into the house.

Thirty-Four

Wait in my study, Mr. Dexter," said the ambassador.

"Sir, this man is a wanted terrorist."

"I am aware of his reputation."

"If he gets violent—"

"I shall call you if I need you."

They went into the living room.

"Can I use the computer?" asked Jake. "There's something I need to show you."

Jake sat down at the computer desk; the others took the sofas. Mr. and Mrs. Knight were regarding Yakuuba with a mixture of interest and terror, as if an unknown species of rattlesnake had suddenly poked its head up in their bath.

"You've got a nerve coming here," said Mr. Knight in French.

Yakuuba inclined his head. "I had no choice," he said. "If I had not come, you would not have believed my innocence."

"Why should you care what we believe?"

"Because where your beliefs go, planes and guns follow close behind."

"I see. You came here to save your own skin."

The outlaw stared in disbelief. He stood up without a word and walked toward the door.

"Wait," said Mr. Knight. "Forgive me—I spoke rashly."

Yakuuba stopped, his hand on the door handle. He turned around, and his eyes blazed with anger. "I came here to save many skins, *monsieur*, my own included."

"I apologize," said Mr. Knight.

"*Your children's included.*"

"I know. Come and sit down."

"I wish to stand."

"Very well. What do you believe is going on here?"

"It's obvious," said the outlaw. "Someone is playing a trick on you. It is a very old trick. Here in Africa we call it the elephant dance."

"Go on."

"One day, Al Hajji Lion decided to rid his forest of mice. He was far too old and slow to chase after them himself, so instead he invited all the elephants in his forest to a dance. Al Hajji Lion was a very cunning cat, *monsieur*. He knew that when elephants dance, mice get trampled."

There was a long silence in the room, broken eventually by Jake. "Come and have a look at this," he said. "I just downloaded it from Facebook. It's the video I took at the gold banquet the other night. Look, that's one of the men who kidnapped us. In this clip he's dressed as a waiter, but we saw him yesterday in Djibo, and he's actually a *gendarme*."

"And look who he's talking to," said Kas.

"That clip proves nothing," said Mr. Knight. "People talk to waiters about all sorts of things. He was probably ordering a cocktail."

"Yeah, right," said Jake. "A cocktail with a really long name."

The ambassador tutted and raked a hand through his graying hair. "I refuse to believe that Beogo is behind all this. He was very upset by your abduction."

"I'll bet he was even more upset by our rescue," muttered Jake.

There was a knock on the front door. "Ambassador Knight," boomed a voice. "Open up, *s'il vous plaît*!"

"Here we go," muttered Kas. "It's Al Hajji Lion himself."

Mr. Knight went into the hall and opened the front door. "*Bonjour*, Commissioner Beogo! Come and celebrate with us. Our children are free." He ushered the policeman into the living room.

Beogo forced a smile, but his eyes were cold. "*Salut*, children," he said in French. "Good to see you again. Sunburned but unharmed, I see."

The ambassador smiled and rubbed his hands. "Commissioner, would you like a cup of Darjeeling?"

"No, thank you. I would like that man over there." The police commissioner pointed at Sor, and there was undisguised hatred in his eyes.

The ambassador nodded vaguely. "I was just telling Yakuuba how grateful I am to him. It was he who brought the children back, you see."

"He is a bandit."

"He is our guest."

"Not anymore." Beogo opened a pair of handcuffs.

The ambassador glided in between the police commissioner and the outlaw. "Commissioner, I beg you not to be hasty."

"*Désolé, Ambassadeur.* I have pursued this man for many years, and now at last I intend to arrest him."

"I forbid it."

"*Forbid?*" The police commissioner curled his lip.

"You forget that this embassy is sovereign British territory. Yakuuba Sor has claimed temporary refuge, and I have granted it."

"Stand aside, Ambassador. I'm warning you."

Mr. Knight placed a hand on the policeman's arm and smiled amiably. "Commissioner, we have a fascinating new lead on the identity of the kidnapper. We have a video clip from Tuesday night's banquet, and it clearly shows one of the waiters—"

"We already know the identity of the kidnapper," said Beogo, shaking off the ambassador's hand. "And kidnapping is the *least* serious of the charges that we shall be bringing against him."

"The courts will decide," said Mr. Knight stiffly. "In the meantime, Commissioner, perhaps you should leave."

"Do you realize who you are talking to?" said the police commissioner. "With a single phone call I could have this embassy shut down. I could have you declared persona non grata, and you would be on the next plane back to England with your career in tatters."

The ambassador emitted a nervous laugh. "I trust that will

not be necessary," he said. "We have always been led to believe that our diplomatic presence here is mutually benefi—"

"Quiet!" Beogo waved a hand. "Listen to me carefully, Ambassador, while I tell you what is going to happen. I am going to step outside for five minutes, and you are going to consider your position. If you are wise, you will say your goodbyes to this bandit and you will send him out to us. But if the five minutes elapse and you have still not sent him out, you will force us to violate the dignity of your residence. My men will storm the building and shoot the bandit on sight. We will do our best to ensure the safety of your family, but we cannot guarantee it. Stun grenades can be unpredictable, I find."

So saying, the police commissioner saluted, turned on his heel, and marched out, slamming the front door behind him.

The ambassador sat down heavily on a sofa and clasped his hands between his knees to stop their shaking. No one spoke. The tension in the room was palpable.

It was Jake's mother who broke the silence, and she reverted to English so that Yakuuba would not understand. "On balance," she said, "I think we should send him out."

"No!" cried Jake and Kas in unison.

Mrs. Knight raised a hand. "Quentin," she said, "you heard

what that odious man said. If we don't give them the boy, he's going to storm the building. He wasn't bluffing."

"I know." Mr. Knight picked at a loose stitch on the arm of the sofa. "Is there nowhere we can hide him?"

Jake had once gone on a school trip to Baddesley Clinton, an Elizabethan manor house containing several "priest holes" for fleeing Catholics. With hidden doors in the paneling, secret passageways in the ceiling, and a panic room under the toilet, it was a wonderful place. But even if the embassy house in Ouagadougou had been full of hidey-holes, Jake was sure that Yakuuba would not use them. It was not his style.

Yakuuba strolled to the back window and looked out at the mango tree and the beehives. As he stood there, a black shadow flitted past the window. A shadow with an automatic handgun.

"Did you see that?" said Mrs. Knight. "I don't want to sound hysterical, Quentin, but we have only four minutes left."

Sor turned around and smiled at the Knight family. "Thank you for your hospitality," he said. "I should go now. I have to be back at my camp by morning."

In the silence that followed, Jake had a wild urge to laugh. How could Yakuuba be so cool while this tornado was raging around him? How could he talk about going back to his camp when it was obvious he would not get as far as the front gate?

"Before I go," said Yakuuba, "I will take my reward."

"What do you mean?" said Mr. Knight.

"The reward for the safe return of your children. The reward you announced on the radio."

The ambassador wrung his hands. "Surely you would rather we kept your reward here for you," he said. "If I give it to you now, the police will simply take it off you when they—"

"Nevertheless," interrupted Sor, "I will take it now."

"Three minutes left," said Mrs. Knight. "For goodness' sake, just give the boy what he wants. It's worth every penny just to get rid of him."

"Very well." The ambassador hurried out of the room.

Kas rounded on her mother, white with fury. "*Just to get rid of him!* Am I going mad or did you actually *say* that? This boy risked his life for me and Jake, but you couldn't give a monkey's. You just want to give him his money and throw him to the wolves. Much easier."

"Kirsty Knight, how dare you! It's you I'm trying to protect."

"Me and the living-room carpet, right? If the police storm

the building, they might get carried away in the excitement and forget to take their boots off at the door."

"Kirsty, hold your tongue! This is police business, and if Beogo intends to arrest your friend, then we have no power to stop him."

"You're wrong." Kas laughed bitterly. "You're so wrong it stinks. Open up the windows, quick, and let some of the wrong out."

"Kirsty Knight, go to your room this minute."

"No chance. If you're sending Yakuuba out there, I'm going with him."

Mr. Knight came back in clutching a bulging envelope, followed by an angry-looking Dexter.

"You're not seriously going to give him that, are you?" the spy asked. "The boy will be dead in five minutes, and any money on his person will be confiscated by the police."

"We don't know that," said Mr. Knight, handing the envelope to Yakuuba. "All we know is he brought Jake and Kirsty back to us, and this is his reward."

Yakuuba took the envelope and counted it. "Thank you," he said. "May I take your bee suit as well, Madame Knight?"

"Pardon?"

"The bee suit in the corner there."

"They won't fall for that," said Jake anxiously. "They'll know it's you as soon as they see you."

"Take it," said Mrs. Knight. "Take whatever you want. Just get out!"

"*Merci.*" Yakuuba put on the overalls, the boots, the gloves, and the face protector. "I need my slingshot, too," he said. "You took it off me in the yard."

Dexter threw it to him. "One slingshot versus thirty automatic handguns," he sneered. "I don't fancy your chances, boyo."

Sor scooped up a handful of pebbles from a potted plant in the corner of the room. "*Au revoir,* Jake," he said.

"Goodbye," said Jake.

"*Au revoir, princesse.*"

Kas tried to reply but was too choked up.

"Your time is up!" shouted Beogo, pounding on the front door with a sledgehammer fist. "Is the outlaw coming out, or are my men coming in?"

"He's coming out!" shouted Mr. Knight.

Yakuuba swaggered toward the front door, swinging his shoulders like a cowboy. Then he turned and ran up the stairs.

Dexter chased after him, taking the steps three at a time. "Come back here, you coward!"

"Where's he going?" asked Mrs. Knight. "There's nowhere to hide upstairs."

"I have no idea," the ambassador replied. "He's blinking terrified, poor lad."

Jake shook his head. "He's not trying to hide. He's going back to his camp, just like he said he would."

"But how?" said Mrs. Knight. "There are thirty armed policemen in the compound."

Jake shrugged. "You don't know Yakuuba."

Thirty-Five

The young outlaw sprinted into the back bedroom and over to the window. He opened the window, punched the mosquito screen out of its frame, and climbed out onto the ledge. There below him was a line of policemen. Some of them wore blue berets, marking them out as FIMO, Burkina Faso special forces.

The mango tree was right in the middle of the backyard, and its outermost branches were three horse lengths from the window. Yakuuba took a deep breath and coiled himself for the leap of his life.

"You'll never make that jump!" The voice belonged to Dexter. "It's too far away. You'll splatter yourself all over the—"

Dexter was silenced midsneer by his enemy's slingshot, a single stone that split his lip and broke two front teeth.

The outlaw turned and jumped, pushing off the window

ledge as hard as he could. He sailed through the air, reached out for a branch, missed it, and grabbed the next. The branch swayed violently, sending a heavy rain of mangoes pattering onto the ground. There were shouts below and the crack of a pistol. Game on.

Yakuuba swung from branch to branch: forward, down, forward, down, forward, and down again into the fork of the tree, where the branches were thick and the leaves dense. As soon as he was sure of his footing, he splayed his arms like a tightrope walker and half walked, half ran along the opposite branch. Bullets shredded the leaves around him and spattered against the tree trunk. Sor dropped to the ground and rolled to break his fall.

"Shoot to kill!" shouted Beogo. "Don't let him escape!"

The beehives. Yakuuba dodged behind the first one and tried to make himself small. Bullets tore into the hive, riddling the wood and honeycomb with daylight. A furious buzzing came from within.

The policemen advanced, their pistols set to automatic, strafing the beehive with lead until it began to disintegrate. Blood pounded in Yakuuba's ears. He sprinted five yards to the second hive and dived behind it.

Commissioner Beogo was the first to realize the danger. He

knew full well that bees hate any disturbance of their hives, and that loud noise or vibration agitates them even more. "Hold your fire!" he shouted. "I repeat, do not fire on the hives!"

His warning came too late. Two boiling, frenzied columns of worker bees rose from the ruptured hives and swelled into a thick black cloud. They swarmed toward the home wreckers, barbed stings at the ready, apoplectic with rage.

"Stand your ground, men!" hissed Beogo. "Remember your training."

Yakuuba flattened himself against the back of the third hive and pulled the mesh visor down over his face as the fury descended on him. Bees shrieked in his ears and tried to sting him through his protective clothes and gloves and the mesh of his face guard.

Beogo's men did not have the benefit of protection, and they stood in wide-eyed horror as the bees enveloped them. Elite fighters they may have been, but they were also townies. They did not know bees. There were shouts of fear and pain as two thousand irate insects alighted on ears and nostrils and necks and lips, stinging fast and hard. *Gendarmes* were shouting, running, whirling their arms like windmills, trying to bat the homicidal insects away.

"Calm yourselves!" yelled Beogo. "If they smell your fear, that makes it worse. Stop flapping your arms. Focus on the outlaw. Find an angle. Six bottles of pastis to the man who nails him!"

Lieutenant Ouedraogo dropped to the ground and began to move forward in a fast cat crawl. Followed closely by four of his best men, he advanced toward the third hive, ignoring the red-hot jabs of pain all over his body. He narrowed the angle bit by bit, and *there it was,* the outlaw's head, poking out from behind the hive.

"Get in here!" Jake's mum was shouting from the house. "Get inside, all of you. You're going to get stung to death!"

The lieutenant propped himself up on one elbow and lined up his sights. The masked head of the outlaw disappeared, a gloved hand shot out, and a whole tray of honeycomb came skimming across the ground toward him, spilling its occupants as it came. The air swirled with dust and yet more angry worker bees. The lieutenant cringed and writhed. It was impossible now to get the outlaw in his sights, let alone to fire a shot.

"Twelve bottles!" roared Beogo. "A whole case of pastis to the man who takes him down!"

But the lieutenant was no longer thinking about pastis. The

pain on his face and neck was too much to bear. He jumped to his feet, sprinted to the swimming pool, and dived in fully clothed. As he entered the water, the thick layer of bees peeled off him, but they did not fly away. They hovered there, just above the surface of the water, waiting for their victim to come up for air as he surely must.

"Get out of the pool!" shouted Jake's mum. "Into the house, all of you!"

Sor was on the move again, dragging the hive with him as a shield. He set it down next to the shed and peered over the top, scanning the situation.

The *gendarmes* no longer cared about their mission. Each of them was flapping and dancing in his own private hell. One by one they turned and ran for the house.

Except for one. François Beogo was striding toward him, revolver in hand, his face covered with exultant bees. On he came, squinting at his prey through puffed-up eyelids.

Yakuuba ducked down and fitted a pebble into his slingshot. Then he leaped up and slung the pebble, chinning the police commissioner and knocking him off balance. He climbed up onto the hive, fired another stone, and jumped up onto the shed roof.

Lying in the dust, Commissioner Beogo rattled off the contents of his magazine. One of the rounds tore through the outlaw's face guard and grazed the side of his head, but it was only a skin wound. Yakuuba slung two more pebbles, vaulted the wall of the compound, and disappeared from view.

Thirty-six

Commissioner Beogo, can you hear me?"

Jake's mum knelt on the ground next to the stricken police commissioner. She loosened his belt and undid the brass buttons on his uniform jacket. Beogo and three other men had received more than a hundred stings each and were in very serious condition.

The bees that had delivered their stings littered the ground, dead or dying. The others, sensing a threat to their colony, had swarmed and left the premises.

"That dirty terrorist . . . will get what he . . . deserves," wheezed Beogo in English. His eyes were swollen shut and he seemed to be having difficulty breathing. "He's destined . . . for hellfire."

"Stay still," said Mrs. Knight. She was using her long nails to scrape the bee stingers out of Beogo's skin, starting with those on his face and neck. "You are in shock, and you need an adren-aline injection. The ambulance is on its way."

"All of them . . . destined . . . for hellfire," croaked the po-lice commissioner. His eyes rolled up into his head and his whole body began to spasm violently.

"What's going on?" asked Jake. "What's he saying?"

Mrs. Knight jumped and looked up at her son. "I didn't see you there," she said. "Please don't watch this, Jake—it'll give you nightmares. Go back in the house."

The ambulances finally arrived. They took nineteen *gendarmes* to a local hospital for treatment. Beogo and two others were taken directly to the morgue.

The rest of the *gendarmes* left on foot, limping and leader-less, shaking their heads in disbelief at what they had just seen: thirty armed men beaten in a pitched battle by one boy with a slingshot. Some of them covered their embarrassment with vague threats against the British embassy.

When the last *gendarme* had left the compound, the Knight family held a hurried conference in the study.

"I've just been on the phone to the Foreign Office," said Jake's father. "I asked for permission to close the embassy and evacuate."

"What did they say?" asked Jake.

"They want the embassy to stay open, but they recommend that you and Kirsty be sent home to England for a while."

Kas gasped. "This is my home," she said. "I don't know anyone in England."

"Nevertheless, there is still a significant kidnapping risk. Your mother and I think that—"

"No way." Kas had tears in her eyes. "I'm not going."

"Yes, you are," said Mrs. Knight, and the tone of her voice made it clear that argument was useless.

"There is a flight tonight from Ouagadougou to London," said Mr. Knight. "Aunt Rosemary will meet you at the airport, and you can stay with her until things calm down. I'll go and call her now." He hurried out of the room.

"And I'm going to make a pot of tea," said Mrs. Knight, heading for the door. "Go upstairs and pack your bags, you two, then come down and set the table."

"How long do we have to stay with Aunt Rosemary?" asked Jake.

"Not long," replied his mum brightly. "Just until things here quiet down a bit."

She left them alone in the study, reeling from the news of their imminent evacuation.

"Typical," said Jake.

Kas flopped into a swivel chair and spun moodily from side to side. "I'd rather stay with the Friends of the Poor again than with Aunt Rosemary."

"Don't let Dad hear you talking like that. He'll have you treated for Stockholm syndrome."

Kas suddenly stopped swiveling. "What's that?"

"It's where a hostage falls in love with—"

"No, what's that?" Kas was pointing at something in the wastepaper basket underneath the study desk.

Jake looked and saw a shimmer of red. He bent down and rummaged in the basket. "It's a beetle," he said, picking it up. "Or at least it used to be. It's been mangled."

"Gross," said Kas.

"It's that robot beetle we saw in Kongoussi."

"The one Dexter was using to track us?"

"Yes, it's got some sort of GPS component. At least it did have. Looks like someone has cut it out."

"Dexter," said Kas. "He's only happy when he's maiming and killing."

"Come on." Jake threw the mangled cyborg back in the wastebasket. "We should go and pack."

It took them half an hour to pack their bags, twenty minutes to shower, and five minutes to set the table for the evening meal.

The fried chicken was very tasty, much better than *nyiiri*, but the atmosphere around the table was unbearably heavy. Mr. and Mrs. Knight had many questions about Jake and Kas's kidnapping and their journey home, but Jake was far too tired to talk about it properly, and Kas was far too angry.

It was a relief when Dad pushed back his chair and announced that it was about time they all got going to the airport. "I'll give you one last ride on the Dakar," he said to Jake. "Your mother and sister will follow in the car with the luggage."

Twenty minutes later the motorcycle shot out of the gates and roared along Embassy Row, heading for the airport. Jake hung on to the pillion grips and tried to fix the sights and sounds of Ouagadougou in his memory. As they passed the president's palace, he lifted his visor and leaned over to talk to his father. "Where's Dexter? I haven't seen him since the bee thing."

"I think he went to look for a dentist," said Mr. Knight. "Sor broke two of his teeth as a parting gift."

"Serves him right."

Mr. Knight shook his head. "Jake, I know you don't like

Roy Dexter, but he's not a bad man. He saved your friend's life this afternoon."

"How do you work that out?"

"When I went into my study to get Yakuuba's reward, Roy was sitting there mending his slingshot for him. He said the rubber had come loose and he was retightening it. Just think, if it had broken in the middle of the bee battle, would he still have gotten away?"

"Why would Dexter mend Yakuuba's slingshot?" asked Jake. "He hates Yakuuba."

"There's nowt as queer as folk," his dad replied. "Anyway, here we are. Ouagadougou International Airport. Gateway to heaven."

They left the Dakar in the parking lot and waited for Jake's mum and Kas to turn up with the luggage. When the car finally arrived, the family had to run all the way to the check-in desk, and even then they only just made it on time.

The clerk behind the desk began to make a fuss about two minors traveling unaccompanied, but when she saw their green diplomatic passports, she changed her tune. She apologized profusely and even asked if they would like free use of the VIP lounge.

"No," said Jake. "We want to be with everyone else."

"How many pieces of luggage do you have?" asked the clerk.

"One each."

"Did you pack them yourselves?"

"Yes."

"Have you got a tag?"

"What?" Jake stared at her.

"A luggage tag, to write your destination address. Have you already got one?"

A tag. In his mind's eye Jake was back in the study, looking at the mangled beetle. . . . *It's got some sort of GPS component. At least it did have. Looks like someone has cut it out.*

"Come on, Jake," said Mr. Knight. "The lady asked you a question."

Roy was mending Yakuuba's slingshot for him. He said the rubber had come loose and he was retightening it. . . .

"Jake," repeated Mr. Knight, "do you need a luggage tag?"

That's a slingshot. He takes it with him everywhere. . . .

"Are you all right, Jake?" said Mrs. Knight. "You look ever so pale."

All of them . . . destined . . . for hellfire.

"What's Hellfire?" asked Jake out loud.

"I beg your pardon?"

"It's something military, isn't it? Kas, have you got your phone there?"

"Yes," said Kas.

"Google Hellfire. Look for weapons."

Kas ran the search and scrolled down the list of results. She squealed in horror.

"What does it say?"

"'Hellfire, brackets missile,'" read Kas. "'The Hellfire AGM-114N missile is an enhanced blast weapon with a thermobaric warhead. The missile can be fired from an Apache attack helicopter or a Predator UCAV (Unmanned Combat Air Vehicle). It has been used with success in Bosnia, Afghanistan, and Iraq.'"

"Here are your boarding passes," said the clerk. "Your flight leaves in half an hour from gate four. *Bon voyage*."

Jake ignored the proffered boarding passes. "What else does it say?"

"'In 2008,'" read Kas, "'Hellfire caused controversy in the United Kingdom when it was found out that hundreds of these munitions had been secretly added to the British Army arsenal.

In the United States experts spent eighteen months debating whether troops could use them without breaking international law. Thermobaric weapons, also known as vacuum bombs, have been condemned as "brutal" by human rights groups. They create a pressure wave which—'" Kas was choking up.

"Which what?" said Jake.

"'Which sucks the air out of victims, shreds their internal organs, and crushes their bodies. Hellfire is the next worst thing to a nuclear explosion.'"

"That's revolting," said Mrs. Knight. "I don't want you reading that sort of thing, Kirsty."

"Your boarding passes," said the clerk, waving them under Jake's nose.

"Dad, you've got to call the Foreign Office," said Jake.

"What on earth for?"

"Roy Dexter took the GPS component out of the cyborg beetle and wound it into the rubber of Yakuuba's slingshot."

The ambassador raised an eyebrow. "That's a little far-fetched, even for you, Jake."

"Think about it," said Jake. "What's the one part of Yakuuba's outfit that never changes, no matter what disguise he's wearing?"

"I really couldn't say."

"His slingshot! Yakuuba takes it everywhere with him. Don't you see, Dad? This was Dexter's plan B, in case Sor found a way to escape. Last thing Beogo said was something about Sor being destined for Hellfire. I'll bet you anything that a Predator UCAV is tracking that slingshot on a GPS receiver right this minute."

"I'm closing check-in," said the clerk. "Do you want these boarding passes or not?"

"No," said Jake.

"Yes," said his father firmly.

Kas's lower lip was trembling. "Yakuuba said he had to be back home by tomorrow morning. He's going to lead the Predator straight to his camp. There are forty teenagers at that camp, Dad. We have to warn them."

"Honestly," said Mr. Knight, "I fail to see—"

"Tell me this, Dad," said Jake. "Does Burkina Faso have the Hellfire missile in its artillery?"

"Certainly not."

"What if Britain were requested to donate a missile?"

"Thankfully, we are not in the habit of donating missiles."

"Not even to destroy a known terrorist training camp?"

Mr. Knight stared at his son for a long time before shaking his head. "I'm not going to have this conversation with you, Jake. If anything like that were going to happen, I would be the first to know about it."

"Are you sure?" said Jake. "You've been sheltering a wanted terrorist in your embassy all afternoon. Dexter thinks you've gone soft in the head, and the Foreign Office probably agrees with him."

"How dare you!"

"I'm sorry, Dad, but we've got to warn Yakuuba. The Ministry of Defense is sending a Predator to obliterate his camp."

Mr. Knight took the boarding passes from the airline clerk and pressed them into Jake's hand. "You are upset," he said, "and you have every reason to be. You have been through more this week than anyone could expect you to cope with. You need calm and rest, and you will get those things with Aunt Rosemary."

"But Dad—"

"Not another word, Jake. Say goodbye to your mother."

If Mr. Knight felt even a twinge of unease, he was not showing it. It was pointless to persist. Jake took the boarding passes and shouldered his backpack.

"Bye, Mum," he said, hugging her. Then he held out his arms and hugged his father. "Bye, Dad."

"Take care, son," said his father.

"Isn't this cozy?" said Kas. "Forgive me if I don't join the hug fest, won't you? I think the hypocrisy would suffocate me."

"Goodbye, princess," said Mr. Knight. "I'm sorry you're hurting."

"It's all relative," said Kas. "I'd be hurting even more if I had a Hellfire missile dropped on my head." She turned away, picked up her hand luggage, and half walked, half ran toward Departures. Jake hurried to catch up.

Kas was furious. "I can't believe you bottled it," she said. "It looked like you were standing up to him and then suddenly you just gave up."

"He wasn't buying it," said Jake. "I could have talked till my tongue fell off—it wouldn't have done any good."

They went through passport control and security and on into an air-conditioned departure lounge. There was no point sitting down—people were already lining up at the departure gate with their passports and boarding cards ready for inspection. Jake and Kas joined the back of the line.

"And what's with the hugging?" said Kas. "I haven't seen you hug Dad since you were, like, four years old."

"You're right," said Jake. "But this time there was a very good reason for hugging." He took his right hand out of his pocket and jangled the keys to his father's motorcycle.

Kas's eyes widened. "Who do you think you are, the Artful Dodger? What are you going to do with those?"

"Isn't it obvious? I'm going to go and warn Yakuuba. If I take the Dakar, I might even beat him back to the camp."

"You're not serious."

"Never been more serious in my life."

"But you've never driven Dad's bike."

"I've watched how Dad does it," said Jake. "I've got a pretty good idea of the controls."

"You don't know where the camp is."

"Yes, I do. Remember how I charged my phone in that grass hut?"

"Yes, but there was no signal."

"No phone signal," corrected Jake. "But the GPS worked just fine."

"You got a fix!" cried Kas.

"And memorized it, just in case. Friends of the Poor: fourteen degrees twenty-one minutes sixteen seconds north, one degree fifty-eight five west."

"I suppose you think you're clever," said Kas.

"Above average, yes."

"And you're seriously planning to take Dad's bike and ride it back up north?"

"Thought I might."

Kas looked at him, and for the first time in ages there was admiration in her eyes. "You know what you are?" she said.

"What?"

"You're an outlaw."

Thirty-seven

The passengers for flight 938 to London had their passports checked and their boarding cards swiped. Then they were herded aboard a shuttle bus, which would take them the short distance to the waiting plane.

Jake and his sister sat at the back of the bus. Jake's palms were sweating. It was not too late to abandon his madcap plan. If he chose to, he could simply hand Dad's bike keys to an airline official, get on the plane, and be back in England in time for breakfast. He thought of Aunt Rosemary's ivy-covered country cottage and he could almost smell the sizzling bacon.

Then he thought of Yakuuba, and his resolve returned. Here at last was the opportunity to go on an adventure that meant something, an adventure that wasn't all about himself.

He borrowed Kas's phone and rang his father.

"Hello, princess."

"Dad, it's me," said Jake.

"Hello, son, are you on the plane?" Mr. Knight sounded frazzled. There was a definite lost-keys wildness about his voice.

"Almost—we're on the shuttle bus. Kas wanted to say sorry about before. She didn't mean to be horrible."

"Tell her it's fine. Tell her not to worry about it."

"Dad, are you okay? You sound weird."

"I'm all right," said Mr. Knight, "but I have lost my bike keys. I must have dropped them somewhere."

"Where are you?"

"I'm by the bike. Your mum already left in the car."

"Now that you mention it," said Jake, "I think I might have heard some keys fall. I didn't think anything of it at the time."

"Really?" His father's voice was full of hope. "Where was that, Jake?"

"Near the check-in desk," said Jake, wincing as he said it. He tried to tell himself that this was for the best, but still it lingered—the sour, metallic taste of a deliberate lie.

"I'll go and have a look. Thank you, son—I'm glad you called."

Jake hung up and gave Kas her phone. The shuttle bus had

stopped. Passengers were streaming off the bus and up the steps of the waiting airplane.

"I guess this is it," said Kas. "See you around."

"Don't hug me," whispered Jake. "People will think it's weird if they see us saying goodbye here."

"I wasn't going to hug you," said Kas. She stuck out her tongue, jumped off the bus, and started toward the plane.

Jake waited at the back of the bus and watched his little sister hurry up the steps. *Go for it*, he murmured.

At the top of the steps, Kas stopped dead. "I can't do it," she sobbed. "I can't go in there." She was shaking and crying and flapping her hands in front of her face.

The flight attendants at the door of the plane hurried toward Kas, and one of them put a hand on her shoulder. The travelers on the steps below shuffled restlessly and craned their necks to see what the holdup was. With everybody's eyes on his sister's theatrics, Jake hopped off the bus and began to edge backward away from the plane.

Kas was bent over double and clinging tight to the handrails. "I'm scared of flying, innit!" she cried.

A flight attendant was cooing in her ear, trying to move her to one side and let the other passengers through.

But Kas was not ready to be moved aside just yet. "I'm going to throw up!" she shouted, and the flight attendant sprang back out of range.

Nice one, Kas, thought Jake as he melted into the night. *That was the perfect diversion.* He turned and sprinted across the tarmac, grateful for the cover of darkness, taking the shortest route toward the perimeter fence.

It was a chainlink fence, which Jake was not used to. As he ran, he tried to imagine the dynamics of this new surface and how it would affect his wall run. He neared the fence, shortened his stride, and focused on the thin metal bar along the top. He took off powerfully on his right foot and planted his left at chest height. The chainlink mesh was springier than any wall, and Jake used the spring to give extra power to his upward launch.

It worked. He grabbed the horizontal bar, swung himself up and over, slithered down the other side, and landed in an undignified heap on the edge of the parking lot. There was no sign of his father, who must still be in the check-in hall searching for his lost keys.

Half crouching, Jake ran across the parking lot. The Dakar seemed even bigger than he remembered it. It was a monster.

The helmet was in a compartment behind the fuel tank. He put it on and straddled the bike. He could just about reach the gears and the foot brake with his left foot, but he could only touch the ground by leaning the bike slightly to one side. He kick-started the engine, and it rumbled into life. *First gear, open the throttle, let the clutch out slowly.* The bike shot forward.

He rode a quick practice lap of the parking lot to get a feel for gear changes and cornering, then burst out onto the main road. He did not yet feel in control, but that was something he was getting used to. Feeling in control was something he had left behind in England.

The huge Fespaco traffic circle was gridlocked during the daytime, but at night it was clear. Jake braked gently and leaned into the bend. The traffic circle swung him around and spat him out onto Avenue Kwame Nkrumah, epicenter of Ouagadougou nightlife. Hotels, clubs, and restaurants flashed past in a blur of neon. Jake turned left through Place de la Révolution and plunged on into Tampui, one of the poorest districts of Ouaga-dougou.

Jake gunned the throttle hard. Forty kilometers per hour, read the speedometer, then fifty, sixty, seventy. He changed up through the gears, his heart lightened by the dizzying bliss of speed. Eighty, ninety, one hundred . . . Circular huts with thatched roofs flashed past in his headlight. Adrenaline buzzed in his veins.

As he left the city lights behind, Jake leaned forward and plugged the coordinates of the camp into his father's GPS unit. This was the Djibo road, and if all went well, he would reach his destination by sunrise.

Thirty-eight

High in the sky, red kites greeted the dawn with joyous whoops and whistles. As the sun rose over the Chiltern Hills, it illuminated the sweeping fields, dramatic chalk ridges, beech woods, and quaint villages of southeast England.

One such village was Walter's Ash, a sleepy community with a church, a pub, and a cricket field. To the east of the village was Harry's Home of Rest for Retired Horses, one hundred twenty acres of lush pasture. To the west was a very different enclosure, carpeted not with grass but with concrete, and surrounded not by low wooden fences but by high electrified barricades. Armed guards and Belgian shepherd sentry dogs patrolled the perimeter.

This was Strike Command, operational hub of the Royal Air Force, and at its heart was a nuclear bunker housing four top-secret installations. Most secret of all was the PGCS cockpit—Predator Ground Control System. In a dark, air-conditioned room, two enormous swivel chairs faced an array of glowing monitors and consoles. One chair was marked "Pilot," the other "Sensor."

Sensor operator Shaun Marshall shifted in his chair and took a long swig from a sickly energy drink. In the dead of night his emergency pager had summoned him to Strike Command PGCS, and he had been here ever since. A terrorist training camp had been located on the edge of the Sahara Desert, and Predator 107 had been dispatched to deal with it. *Deal with it,* he mouthed, and the corner of his mouth twitched upward. His superiors used such quaint euphemisms.

He glanced across at his colleague in the Pilot chair, the impish Susie Cray. No one could accuse Susie of being quaint. She had been piloting Predators for ten years and was under no illusions about what her job entailed. "Blitz it," "smash it," "smoke it," "flatten it"—in matters of destruction Susie Cray was a human thesaurus. Technically, however, the act of destruction belonged not to Pilot but to Sensor. Tonight, as always, the finger on the red button was his.

Susie caught his eye and smirked. "Looks like Target One

has taken pity on you, Sensor," she said. "He must have heard what a terrible shot you are. Why else would he hide in a marquee with an enormous red cross painted on the roof?"

Shaun chuckled and looked back at his screens. Three widescreen monitors at eye level showed a full-motion video image of the camp below, with the target marquee clearly visible in the center. Below that were three smaller screens: radar, laser designation, and the view from the nose cam. The job of a sensor operator was to control these cameras, fire the laser designator and missiles, and communicate with the intelligence specialists of MI6.

Target 1, the terrorist with the GPS tag, had arrived at the desert camp more than an hour ago. He had entered the marquee, and since then nothing more had been seen of him. Shaun had used a satellite datalink to upload video of the camp to Bluebird, the MI6 operative in charge of the operation. Now the Predator was in "standby mode," waiting for a decision as to whether or not they were indeed looking at a terrorist camp.

"What's that?" said Susie, eagle-eyed as ever. "Unidentified vehicle entering camp to the south."

"Sensor copies," replied Shaun. "Large motorcycle on the move and approaching target marquee. One rider, unidentified.

Motorcycle stopping outside marquee. Rider dismounting. Rider entering marquee."

"It's only five thirty in the morning," drawled Susie. "Bit early for visitors."

A blue light flashed on Shaun's console, signaling an incoming communication. He pressed a button next to the flashing light and spoke into his headset microphone. "This is Sensor 107, receiving."

"Sensor 107, this is Bluebird," said a posh male voice. "Positive ID on the Predator 107 reconnaissance pictures. London confirms that your location is a training camp for terrorists, over."

"Sensor copies."

"Confirm your weapons loadout, Sensor 107."

"Two Hellfire missiles, Bluebird."

"Copy that. Deploy one missile to destroy the camp, over."

"Sensor copies."

"Fire at your discretion."

"Sensor copies, over and out."

The joysticks in Shaun's hands and the pixelation of the infrared image made this procedure feel like an old-fashioned video game. But the bomb he was about to drop was very real indeed. As were the people in the camp. This was going to be his sixteenth drop, and it was just as scary now as it was the very first time.

The missile itself consisted of a container of fuel and two separate explosive charges. On release the missile would fall toward the ground, adjusting its course to home in on its laser designator. A hundred meters from the ground, the first explosive charge would burst open the container and a dense cloud of fuel would disperse across the entire camp. The second charge would then ignite the cloud. In a wide-open space like this, the blast wave would be immense. The target marquee would implode immediately like an aerosol can in a bonfire. The massive tree in the center of the camp would be reduced to a pile of cinders. Anyone within five kilometers of the blast center would implode or asphyxiate.

"You're looking a bit peaky there, Sensor," drawled Susie.

"I'm fine," said Shaun. *At least, I will be,* he thought, *once the prelaunch checklist starts.*

There were two checklists to go through. The prelaunch checklist was for the laser designator; the launch checklist was for the missile itself.

"Let's go then," said Susie. "PRF code?"

"Entered."

"AEA power?"

"On."

"AEA bit?"

"Passed."

"Weapon power?"

"On."

"Weapon bit?"

"Passed."

"Code weapons."

"Coded."

"Weapon status?"

"Weapon ready."

"Prelaunch complete," said Susie. "Go ahead and fire the laser designator."

Thirty-nine

The gray light of dawn filtered through the curtains of the embassy bedroom, where Mr. and Mrs. Knight had spent hours in anxious discussion and fretful half sleep. Mrs. Knight had finally gotten to sleep at three o'clock in the morning, but the ambassador was still wide-awake and staring gloomily at the ceiling. It was a great relief that Jake and Kirsty were homeward bound, but the new worry was the security of the British embassy. Would the surviving members of FIMO blame the embassy for yesterday's humiliation, and if so, what terrible revenge might they be preparing?

Then there was the matter of his precious Dakar—a glorious beast of a bike that had simply vanished into thin air. If he ever caught up with that blinking thief, he would make him wish he'd— *What's that sound?*

A sudden creak from down the hall made the ambassador's blood run cold, but it was only the taps being turned on in the guest bathroom. Roy Dexter, another source of worry. A monster, Jake had called him. Was it possible that his son was right? Could Dexter really have persuaded the Ministry of Defense to send a Predator to Sor's camp? The ambassador tutted at the very thought of it. Yakuuba Sor was a thorn in the side of the Burkina Faso authorities, but he was clearly no terrorist—more of a Robin Hood, by the look of him. *If it turns out that Dexter has sent the hawks to Sor's camp,* vowed Mr. Knight, *I will see to it personally that he never works for MI6 again. The only gun he'll be using will be a pricing gun for stocking shelves in his local supermarket.*

His thoughts were interrupted by the opening bars of Beethoven's Fifth Symphony sounding from the cell phone on the bedside table. He picked it up.

"Knight speaking."

"Quentin!" His sister's voice on the other end of the line was strained and tearful. "I don't know what to do. Kirsty is here, but Jake is not!"

"Don't be alarmed, Rosemary—that's typical of our Jake. He almost always gets held up at customs. The harder he tries to look innocent, the guiltier he—"

"No, you don't understand. Kirsty says that he never got on the plane in the first place!"

"What?"

"He's still in Burkina Faso, Quentin. He took your motorcycle. Kirsty says he's gone back to Yakuuba's camp, whatever that means."

Mr. Knight sat bolt upright in bed. "Put her on the line," he snapped.

Forty

The Red Cross marquee was empty save for a solitary figure in the corner.

"*Salaam aleykum,*" said Jake, hurrying toward him.

"*Aleykum asalaam,* " replied Yakuuba. He was sitting cross-legged on the ground next to a kerosene lamp, the only light source in this vast, dark space. "You should not have come, *tuubaaku.*"

"Your slingshot," panted Jake. "I had to come and warn you. There is a tag on your slingshot."

Yakuuba reached into his pocket and took out a tiny black disc.

Jake stared at the tracker tag. "You found it already?"

Yakuuba nodded. "During that fight outside the embassy, a lot of my stones were hitting their targets a centimeter too low.

When that starts happening, you know that your slingshot is wrongly weighted."

Incredible, thought Jake. *That chip must weigh only a couple of grams at most.* "It's a GPS tracker," he said out loud. "It means the *tuubaakus* and the police can follow your every movement."

"Clever." Yakuuba put the disc back in his pocket. "I thought it might be something like that."

"So why bring it back to the camp?" Jake felt a sudden surge of anger. "You've played right into your enemies' hands. Now they know exactly where you and your people are!"

"I wanted them to," said Yakuuba. "I am waiting for them. And you, *tuubaaku*, should leave while you have the chance. This is not your battle."

"I'm staying," said Jake. "And if you've got the idea that there's going to be some kind of epic battle here, you can forget it. The biggest swarm of bees in the world couldn't save you now. Your entire camp is going to be destroyed in the blink of an eye by one horrific bomb."

Yakuuba rested his chin on his hands and smiled. "One day," he said softly, "Yakuuba Sor will be sitting in his tent, and he will hear the sound of a skyboat. He will go outside and he will lift his gaze and he will wonder why that skyboat is flying so low. And that will be the last thought he ever thinks, for Death will swiftly fall upon his head like mango rain from a clear sky."

"You're a maniac," said Jake. "If you've already given up on life, then fine, but don't make all your friends here die with you. We have to wake them all up and evacuate."

"They've gone already," said Yakuuba. "I gave the evacuation order yesterday morning, before we left for Ouagadougou. I have a good nose for danger, my friend. As soon as I heard on the radio that I was wanted for kidnapping two *tuubaakus*, I knew that it was time for the Friends of the Poor to relocate."

Jake reeled. "Where have they gone?"

"Another secret location," said Yakuuba. "They will be able to make a new start, and Mariama will be their leader. Thanks to the reward your father gave me, they now have sufficient funds to set up a new camp. I left the money with Hassan and Husseyni when I passed through Djibo last night."

"So there's nobody left here?"

"Just me," said Yakuuba. "And now you."

"Yakuuba, you have to listen to me," said Jake. "I've got my dad's motorcycle outside. If you come with me now, there might still be time for us to get away."

The outlaw shook his head. "Thank you for your kindness," he said. "But this time the police must get their man."

"Why must they? You are cleverer than any of them, and quicker. You told me yourself, the hero of most African folk-tales is not the lion or the bear, but the rabbit. You can continue to fight!"

"And how many more people would choke in the dust of that fight? People like Dr. Saudogo and Abdul, whose only crime was to be in the same place as me."

"Those people gave their lives to protect you," said Jake. "They thought your life was worth saving, didn't they? This country is full of pain and injustice, of course it is, but you give people hope. Why do you think I came here?"

Yakuuba sighed. "It's Beogo," he said. "He wants me so badly, he's completely out of control. If a man kidnaps *tuubaaku* teenagers today, just imagine the evil he will do tomorrow."

"Beogo won't be doing anything tomorrow. He's dead."

Yakuuba looked up sharply. "Are you sure?"

"Died of his bee stings, right in front of me. Now are you coming with me or not?"

"You are a good friend, *tuubaaku*," replied Yakuuba, and for a moment Jake thought he saw tears in the outlaw's eyes. "I thank you for that."

"Fine, no problem, let's get out of here."

"No." Yakuuba leaned back on his elbows. "You go, *tuubaaku*. I am too tired to run anymore."

Jake stood over the Chameleon and clenched his fists. He wanted to shout, rage, grab the outlaw by his collar, drag him to the bike. But a wrestling match here in the marquee would only make things worse. He shrugged and sat down on the ground.

"What are you doing?" said Yakuuba.

"I don't know. I thought I'd keep you company."

Yakuuba nodded gravely. "We're the same, you and I," he said. "We even have the same name."

"I know."

The two Jacobs sat side by side, staring at the lamp. The flame flickered violently as it burned its last few drops of kerosene.

"Men like us do not live till old age," said Yakuuba. "We ignite, we flare up for one short moment, and then we get snuffed out. The important thing, Jake, is not how long we burn but how bright."

We flare up for one short moment. Of course!

Jake jumped to his feet and ran outside.

Forty-one

"**Initiating** launch checklist," said Susie Cray.

"Ready and waiting," murmured Shaun Marshall, his gaze flickering over the monitors before him.

"MTS autotrack," said Susie.

"Established."

"Select weapon."

"Hellfire AGM-114N."

An unwanted image flashed across Marshall's mind—a group of protesters outside the Houses of Parliament, placards bobbing in the air above their heads. UCAVs: UTTERLY COWARDLY AIR VEHICLES read one. THERMOBARIC = BARBARIC! shrieked another.

"Arm missile," said Susie.

"Missile armed."

Shaun's eye was attracted to a sudden movement in the central monitor: a small figure darting out of the marquee and hurrying over to the waiting motorcycle.

"Where are you off to, pal?" breathed Shaun. But the figure was not going anywhere. He seemed to be kneeling down next to the bike.

"Master arm is hot," said Susie. "Fire missile at the count of three."

Shaun gripped the joysticks tight, and his right thumb hovered over the red button. *Perhaps those protesters were right,* he thought. *Press a button in the Chilterns, people die in the Sahara. Can it be fair to fight a war without even turning up for it?*

Fair or not, he knew what he must do. This bomb was going to drop.

"Three . . . two . . . one . . ."

The screen was momentarily obscured by a bright flash.

"Target toasted!" Susie Cray punched the air. "Excellent job."

Shaun stared at the screen. "I haven't fired yet," he said.

"You *what?* What was that explosion?"

"It was a distress flare," said Shaun.

"Squash 'em, quick, before they launch another one!"

"Where would they have got a distress flare?"

"What does it matter, Shaunie? Terrorists are like magpies—they collect all sorts of strange things. Do your job, will you, and put the critters out of their misery!"

Shaun sighed, reached for the joysticks, and put his finger on the fire button. Susie was right, of course. He must suppress his qualms and do the job he was being paid for.

The blue light on the console was flashing. Shaun opened the coms channel and spoke into his headset microphone. "This is Sensor 107, receiving."

"Sensor 107, this is Bluebird. Do not fire on the target! I repeat, do not fire on the target! There is a British national on the ground at target location. It's the son of the British ambassador."

Forty-Two

Vermilion and purple swaths of watercolor dawn bled gradually through the black of night. The sky lightened in the east, and up over the dunes arose a fiery sun. Six o'clock in the morning and still no sign of Hellfire.

The two Jacobs sat outside the Red Cross marquee, eating biscuits and raisins from an emergency ration pack. In the last few minutes, the poor Dakar had been thoroughly disemboweled; tools, glow sticks, bandages, vitamin tablets, and other miscellaneous entrails lay strewn across the sand. For now, though, food and water were all that was needed.

"Ostriches are not like other birds," murmured Yakuuba, running his finger across the surface of a digestive biscuit.

"Go on, try it," Jake said. "Whenever I feel like ending it all, I eat one of those instead. Makes me feel a whole lot better."

The outlaw took one bite of the biscuit and winced.

"Come on," said Jake. "It can't be as bad as a calabar bean."

Yakuuba laughed. "Tell me something," he said. "Did you mean what you said about me giving people hope?"

"Sure," said Jake. "I saw it in Paaté's eyes when you both told me about that duel between you and Beogo. I heard it in Abdul's voice when he sang that stupid song about the cow prison. I felt it in the marquee the other night when you exposed Sheikh Ahmed for what he was. Forty boys and girls throwing goat bones and sandals into the air—they can't all be wrong, can they?"

Yakuuba pressed his fingertips together and looked up at the sky. "I've been thinking," he said. "I'm not sure Mariama is completely ready to lead the Friends of the Poor on her own. If we don't get blown up in the next few minutes, perhaps I should join them at the new camp. I could support Mariama while she gets used to leadership."

"Sure," said Jake. "That might work."

The sun was fully above the horizon now and shining into their eyes. Jake moved over into the shade of the motorcycle. It was going to be another hot day.

"That story about the calabar duel," Yakuuba said. "I lied."

"Really?" Jake looked up sharply.

"Not to you," said Yakuuba quickly. "I lied to Beogo."

"How do you mean?"

"I didn't eat the bean."

"But how did you—"

"Sleight of hand," said the outlaw. "I pretended to swallow it, but I didn't. I put it down my trousers and swallowed a coffee bean instead."

"Clever," said Jake, impressed.

"Not especially. I hate coffee."

From far away to the south came the unmistakable yammer of helicopter blades. The boys sat still and listened as it came closer. There it was, a black speck low in the sky. There was no point running anymore. If it was FIMO, so be it. But Jake suspected otherwise.

They watched the helicopter hack its way through the early-morning sky. It was heading straight toward the Red Cross marquee, nose slanted downward as it powered toward its destination.

Before long it was starting its descent. Jake and Yakuuba closed their mouths tight and shielded their eyes. Great clouds of sand and dust whirled around them as the helicopter touched down. A door opened, and a tall angular figure strode through the dust toward the marquee.

"Blinking Stockholm syndrome!" bellowed a familiar voice. "As soon as we get you back to England, son, you're going to write a whole blinking essay about it."

But the expression on his father's face belied his angry words.

AFTERWORD

In a novel it is not always easy to distinguish fact from fiction. What follows is a brief guide to *Outlaw*—what is real and what is not.

All the towns and villages mentioned in this book are real places. At the time of writing, my family and I live in Djibo in the far north of Burkina Faso. We often travel to Ouagadougou, passing through Burizanga, Kongoussi, and Sogolzi.

Modern Africa is a complex place. It is a continent of hospitality, joy, wisdom, and wit, but at the same time there is immense human suffering and widespread corruption. I have met countless wonderful people in Burkina Faso, but I have also met mayors and councilors seeking to get rich rather than to govern justly, charlatans selling empty promises and worse-than-useless "medicines," grain merchants meeting at night to engage in illegal price fixing, *gendarmes* intimidating civilians and extorting arbitrary "fines," and European and American miners making vast profits by extracting gold in desperately poor regions.

The character of the Chameleon came out of my longing to see more African men and women take an imaginative, nonviolent stand against injustice and corruption. I would stress the word *nonviolent*, because terrorism is on the rise in the Sahel and the Sahara, as in so much of the world. At the time of writing, AQIM (Al Qaeda in the Islamic Maghreb) is increasingly active in Algeria, Mali, and Niger.

Geothimble does not yet exist, but there are plenty of other options for GPS adventurers. You might try confluencing (www.confluence.org) or geocaching (www.geocaching.com).

Sheikh Ahmed's levitation is a Criss Angel trick that can be viewed on YouTube. Also on YouTube is the video "How to charge your iPod using whipped cream and AA batteries" (thanks, zepplinkin).

Mungo Park was a young Scottish explorer who followed the river Niger all the way to its source. His journals, *Travels in the Interior of Africa*, are available free from Mobile Read (www.mobileread.com).

The Chameleon spoke French with Jake, but all of his proverbs are in Fulfulde, one of West Africa's many indigenous languages. Jake's initial rescuer spoke the same language: *mi faamaay* (pronounced "Me Fahm Eye") simply means "I do not understand."

Fulfulde pronunciation is relatively easy. Simply pronounce all

the sounds as they are written, except for the double vowels, which
sound something like this:

aa   the long-drawn-out ah in the sheep sound "baa"

ee   the long vowel sound in "Heeey, what's up?"

ii   the vowel sound in "key"

oo   the vowel sound in "four"

uu   the vowel sound in "cool"

The Mosquito is a siren that drives away teenagers from
no-loitering zones. It whines at a frequency that can be heard only
by young people. The Mosquito ringtone is based on the same idea
and can be downloaded free from www.teenbuzz.org.

UCAVs such as the Predator have been regularly used by
the U.S. military, as has the brutal and controversial Hellfire missile.
And while the HI-MEMS program (cyborg insects created to act as
surveillance droids) may seem like the stuff of science fiction, it is
scarily real, thanks to research at the University of Michigan.

The Ouagadougou cattle drive leaves from Djibo every
Thursday morning. It consists of four men and a hundred or more
cows. I joined them once but got only as far as Kongoussi. You can
read about that on my blog www.voiceinthedesert.org.uk/weblog,
along with stories of my other adventures in West Africa.

Thanks ever so much for choosing *Outlaw*. I do hope you
enjoyed it.